HOLD 'EM, WYNDHAM!

THE WYNDHAM SERIES

The Fighting Scrub
Bases Full
Hold 'Em, Wyndham!

HOLD 'EM, WYNDHAM!

RALPH HENRY BARBOUR

TO
THE MEMORY OF

PERCY DUNCAN HAUGHTON

SKILLFUL PLAYER, INSPIRING LEADER, BRILLIANT
COACH AND GALLANT GENTLEMAN

Originally published in 1925.
Reprinted by Wildside Press, LLC.
Visit us online at wildsidepress.com

CHAPTER I
COACH AND PLAYER

C lif Bingham paused in the doorway, clicked his heels together and gave a military salute.

"Reporting by order, sir."

"No, Bingham, by request." The football coach arose and strode across the floor, hand outstretched. "I can't issue orders until the term starts. Well, how are you?"

"Fine and dandy, Mr. Otis. Don't I look so?"

"Mm, a bit pudgy, I'd say. But we'll work that off you. Sit here. Except Hanbury you're the first of the gang to report. Couldn't keep away any longer, I presume."

"Something of the sort, sir," answered the boy, smiling. "But the whole truth is that it was so plaguey hot in Providence yesterday that I made up my mind to take the first train I could get this morning and reach here without sizzling. How have you been, sir?"

"Oh, pretty fit, thanks. As you remarked, don't I look so?"

"You've got a corking tan," Clif added in envious tones.

"Good Lord, I'm fairly black!" protested the coach. "I had to appear in dinner clothes a couple of evenings ago, and when I had a look at myself in the mirror I almost got cold feet and stayed away from the party. The white shirt made me look like an Indian! You see, it wasn't so apparent as long as I was in sea togs, but once ashore—" He shook his head ruefully.

"That's a sea tan, then," said Clif.

"Yes, a Long Island Sound tan, Bingham. I spent two whole months in dungaree, and particularly disreputable dungaree, too. We slipped into Providence once to get out of a blow, and I'd have looked you up if I'd known where you lived. Well, I could have found that out, I guess. The real reason I didn't look in on you was that I was too lazy to shave and clean up!"

"When was that, sir?"

"Oh, about ten days ago; maybe the nineteenth or twentieth."

"You wouldn't have found me, Mr. Otis. We didn't get back from the other side until the twenty-second."

1

"Oh, abroad, eh? Lucky dog!"

"Father and I went over in July. We had a sort of reunion in Paris in August. You remember Loring Deane, sir?"

"Deane? Yes, indeed. You met him over there?"

"Yes, sir, he and his folks; and Wattles, of course! We all went to Switzerland together and found Tom Kemble and his father at Neuchatel. It was a sort of a date we'd made in the spring. We were all over the shop together, sir, and had a grand time. Tom was more fun than a goat. It was his first trip across, and, of course, he'd never seen the Alps. But you simply couldn't get him to enthuse. Oh, he was all tied up in a knot with it, but he wouldn't let on once! The best you could get out of him was that the Jungfrau reminded him of Orange Mountain, whatever that is, and that Lake Lucerne wasn't in it with Hopatcong, or some such place. I forgot to say that Tom comes from New Jersey!"

"It wasn't necessary," chuckled the coach. "Did Kemble come up with you?"

"This morning? No, sir, he didn't, and he'll probably be fit to be tied, when he gets to the junction and doesn't find me there according to agreement. He's coming up on the train that gets here at one-something. I just couldn't face the trip in such heat as we had yesterday. It was fairly cold in England when we left, and cool coming back, and this weather is awful!"

"I was seven pounds heavier in July, sir," explained Clif. "I'm a lot more than that now, of course, for I haven't done anything for a month but sleep and eat. I guess those seven will stick by me."

"All the better. Fact is, Bingham, I've been wondering how you'd shape as a tackle."

"Tackle!" exclaimed Clif.

"Yes. You see, we're going to need tackles more than ends this fall. I was counting on Raiford, but he's quit school, I hear. So there's only Weldon, Cotter, Coles and Longwell to start with. Well, there's McMurtry, too, but I wouldn't be surprised to see him in the backfield."

"I guess 'Blondy' would make a good back," said Clif reflectively. "Gosh, I'm willing to try, of course, if you want me to, sir, but I don't know much about the position. It's a lot different from end, I suppose."

"Yes, but you can learn it, Bingham. Anyhow, I'd like to try you out at tackle. Of course, if you don't take to it, all right. I certainly don't intend to lose a good end to secure a second-rate tackle. We're sort of long on end material: Drayton, Couch, Adams, Williams, two or three others besides. None of them except Drayton what you'd call top-notchers, maybe, but Couch did well last fall. This is only tentative, you understand. I wanted to hear what you thought of it."

"Well, we'll see. You've got the general build and weight for a tackle, Bingham, and you're fast and you use your head. Hang it, give me a chap who knows his business and has two feet and a pair of hands and I'll chance him anywhere in the line or back of it! Do you know what makes a good tackle or a good center or a good anything, Bingham?"

"I don't know any *one* thing, Mr. Otis."

"I'll tell you, then." The coach's lips set themselves straight and tight for an instant. "Practice, my boy! Hard practice and plenty of it. I'll guarantee to take any fellow in school and, if he is willing to work and do as I tell him, make a football player of him—*if* I can have enough time! It's lack of time, Bingham, that makes hard sledding for a football coach. Think of it! I get hold of you chaps two months, almost to a day, before I have to trot you into the big game! It's not so bad when you've played a couple of years, but when you haven't, when it's all practically new stuff to you, why, man alive, it's work! That's what puts white hairs in a coach's locks. Or—" he ran a brown hand over his head and grinned—"takes 'em out altogether!"

"It isn't much time, is it?" reflected Clif.

"Jordan, sir?"

"Highland. Jordan comes the week after. Here, look it over."

Clif took the typewritten sheet and read:

Oct. 4, Freeburg High School, at Home
Oct. 11, Highland School, at Highland
Oct. 18, Jordan Academy, at Home
Oct. 25, Cupples Institute, at Cupples
Nov. 1, Minster High School, at Home
Nov. 8, Horner Academy, at Horner
Nov. 15, Toll's Academy, at Home

3

"What's this Jordan Academy, sir?" Clif asked, returning the schedule. "Is she supposed to be good?"

"I hope we do, sir. And wouldn't it be wonderful if we did get through this season with a clean slate? You say it's impossible, Mr. Otis, but you don't really mean it, do you? That is, it *could* be done if—well, if we proved good enough!"

"Why, no, it isn't impossible, Bingham. Let's say extremely improbable, instead. We did about as well last season as we can hope to do this. We won seven out of eight games. Of course, it's an easy matter to say that we should have won all eight, that if we had prepared a bit more for Horner, scouted her and got a line on some of those tricky plays she used, we'd have beaten her; tied her at the least. But somewhere in your schedule, at some moment during your season, you let up just a little. It's natural. It's like target shooting. You make nine bull's-eyes and then at the tenth, when one more good shot will give you a perfect score, you miss. You don't know any reason for it, either. You held just as steadily, aimed as before, but you missed. I guess it's the old law of probability getting in its fine work, Bingham. Well, maybe we shouldn't kick if we come through this season as well as we did last. And, after all, the big prize is the Wolcott game."

"Yes," answered Mr. Otis, "it looks promising. There's not a bit of harm in setting out with a good big ambition, Bingham, either. The more you ask for, the more you generally get! So you and I, at least, can treasure the hope of an undefeated team. Going?"

"Yes, sir, I'll have to beat it, I guess. I've got some stuff to get in the village. Then I'll have to be at the station when Tom arrives or he'll never speak to me again!"

Mr. Otis smiled. "Are you together in dormitory?" he asked.

"Yes, we are this year. We've got Number 40 in West. It's a corking room. Tom was with Billy Desmond last year and I roomed with a chap named Treat, but we thought we'd like to get together for this year and next."

"I hope Kemble is going to show up finely this season," said the coach. "He looked promising last fall. Well, three-thirty, Bingham. By the way, if you run across Owens send him to me, will you? He's

4

here somewhere, for he called me up from the school half an hour ago."

"Yes, I will. Well, see you at the field, sir."

CHAPTER II
NEW QUARTERS

F reeburg, Connecticut is like so many other New England towns that to describe it would be a waste of time. A central street, broad and elm-shaded; two blocks of modest buildings devoted to business; old-fashioned residences, generally white, with green blinds, set back from the thoroughfare; a few more modern and much smaller houses tucked around the corners on the side streets; churches, schools, a town hall, a library, a fire house; irritatingly detached from the village proper, a railroad station at which trains bound northward for Massachusetts and southward for New York pause on their way. Not all of them, either, for there are at least two hoity-toity trains that go straight through with only a careless, half-contemptuous shriek for the little town.

For several moments Clif thought Tom Kemble hadn't come, and just when doubt was becoming certainty he spied him. It was, Clif reflected with an affectionate grin, just like Tom to be the last one out of his car and then to descend as though there was all the time in the world! Clif pushed his way across the platform and made a grab at a battered suit case. "Porter, sir? Porter?" he inquired. Tom saw him then, cried "Alphonse! Alphonse!" in a voice that turned many heads his way, dropped the suit case and a bag of golf clubs and threw his arm about Clif, bestowing a resounding smack on the latter's left cheek. But when he would have planted a similar salute on the other cheek the other cheek was out of range.

"Tom, you blamed idiot!" fumed Clif. "Cut it out!"

"*Ah, mon cher ami!*" cried Tom, still clasping Clif tightly. "*Mon petit chou!*"

"Will you shut up?" cried Clif, struggling, amused but annoyed. "Don't be an ass, Tom! Quit it, I tell you!"

Tom quit it, grinning. The custom of embracing and kissing between Frenchmen had made a great hit with Tom during his visit to Paris, and later he and Clif had amused themselves considerably in Switzerland by staging meetings in such public places as station platforms and hotel lobbies. "*Ah, mon cher Alphonse!*" Tom would ejaculate in tones of delighted surprise. "*Mon cher Armande!*" Clif would rejoin ecstatically. Then they would rush together, embrace and kiss, to the great amusement of Loring Deane and the scandalizing of Wattles, his attendant. Sometimes Tom followed with the rest of his French, declaring fervidly that the view was magnificent, asking Clif how he did and ending up with the seemingly unconnected announcement that his window looked into the garden.

Well, that sort of thing had been all right over there, away from home, where folks did pretty much as they pleased, anyhow; but being embraced and kissed on the station platform at Freeburg, Connecticut, U. S. A., was quite another proposition, and Clif looked distinctly uncomfortable as he pushed his way around the corner of the station, followed by the amused stares of his schoolfellows and the excited piping of a newly arrived junior who asked in a shrill voice: "Dad, did you see that boy kiss the other one?"

"*Aller, cocher! Vit, vit!*" he directed. The driver turned a slow, inquiring gaze upon him over a shoulder.

"How's that? Ain't you fellers for the school?"

"Yes," answered Clif. "West Hall. Don't mind this chap. He's nutty." He leaned back and smiled at the nutty one. "Well, how are you?"

"Never better," replied Tom. "Say, what's the colossal idea? Thought you were going to be at the junction, you rotter!"

Clif explained while the taxi bounded schoolwards, and Tom accepted the explanation with a shrug. "Huh," he said. "All right, but you only got what was coming to you back there on the platform, old son. I owed you that!"

"Seen Loring?" asked Clif.

"No, there wasn't time. He telephoned yesterday, though. Wanted me to come up with him, but I knew there'd be a crowd in the car. He's bringing a couple of fellows along, and, of course, his folks and Wattles. Besides, you'd said you'd be at the junction, and there wasn't any way of getting word to you."

"That was sort of low down, my not keeping the date," said Clif; "but I didn't have the courage. Wasn't it frightfully hot on the train?"

"Hot? It was awful! Say, any of the crowd back?"

"I haven't seen any of them, but 'G. G.' says 'Swede's' here. And Guy Owens. Some of them came up with you, didn't they?"

"Four or five. Treader and Sim Jackson and two or three more. How's Mr. Otis?"

"Hale and hearty. Looks like an Indian. All tanned up. Practice at three-thirty, so you'll just have time to bathe and rest up a few minutes."

Tom groaned. "Practice on a day like this? Is the man not so well in his mind, perhaps?"

"Says we can't afford to miss a day, Tom. We're out for big things this year. Going to clean up. Through the season without a defeat; that sort of thing, you know."

"He say that?"

"We—ell, no; but he did say it would be worth trying. I think so, too. 'Wyndham's undefeated eleven!' Sounds pretty good, doesn't it? Say, what's to keep us from making a stab at it?"

"Stab all you please," grumbled Tom. "But we've got about as much chance to do it as——" He hesitated, lacking a simile, and was spared further effort by the arrival of the taxi in front of the dormitory.

The school stands well back from the streets, from the principal thoroughfare of the town, Oak Street, which runs along the western side of the grounds, and from Elm Street which lies to the south. From Elm Street one looks across a gently rising expanse of excellent turf, and over a long bed of scarlet sage and white cosmos, straight into the little courtyard. On the right is the front end of East Hall, on the left the corresponding elevation of West. The old building is known now as Middle Hall. But one doesn't approach from our present point of view. Instead, a curving drive, shaded by a double row of maples, leads from the junction of the two streets. Here a pair of stone posts, surmounted by globular lights, indicates the way. Up this graveled drive the rattling flivver had sped, to stop, as is the manner of such vehicles, with disconcerting suddenness, in front of the first pair of wide stone steps.

Clif and Tom struggled out, Tom paid the driver—adding a ten-cent tip and the seemingly irrelevant statement, "*Ma fenêtre donne sur le jardin*"—and they went up the steps, occupied by several hesitant youths and a number of bags, and entered West Hall.

"Welcome home," murmured Clif.

"Well, at that," remarked Tom above the clatter of his shoes on the stone treads, "getting back doesn't seem so bad, Clif."

"Bad? I'll say it doesn't! I was tickled to death to get here. Say, Number 40 is all right, Tom. You see for a thousand miles from the rear window!"

"*Le coup d'oeil est magnifique*," agreed Tom.

They climbed two flights to reach Number 40, passed a dozen other rooms, turned finally to the left and were there. Tom slid his bag along the floor, Clif tossed the golf clubs onto a bed and they sank into chairs to mop their faces and inspect the new quarters. Clif had already taken possession of his half—first arrival had given him choice of sides—and his brushes and comb and soap box and other gimcracks were neatly arranged on the fresh white cover atop his chiffonier. There were two framed portraits there, besides; one of his mother, long since dead, and one of his father. Tom noted and sighed.

"Yes, I thought of that," said Clif. "But they're worth it. Each of us has his own, you see."

"Yes, but which is mine?" asked Tom suspiciously.

"Well, I selected this side of the room," replied Clif carelessly, "so I suppose you take the window seat nearest your bed."

"Sounds all right," muttered the other; "but I'll bet there's a catch to it somewhere!" He studied the situation frowningly. Then: "Oh, yes," he exclaimed sarcastically, "I get the north window, eh? Fine in winter, what?"

Clif laughed. "Not so good in winter, Thomas; but think of the long, dreamy days of spring! And look at it to-day. Your window's nice and shady and has a breeze—"

"Breeze!" protested Tom.

"—While mine's got the sun full on it. You see, don't you? You know I wouldn't take advantage of you, old thing."

"No, you wouldn't! What time is it? I'm going to have a ger-lorious shower right now! Say, did you get the stuff out of the storeroom?"

"I did, sir. Everything's attended to. You'll find your togs hanging in your closet, your shoes on the shelf—By the way, Tom, I hate to tell you, but you need a new pair of brogans."

"Heck, do I? Life's just one expense after another! All right. Got a towel? Mine are in the trunk. Thanks. Where's your bath robe?"

"In my closet. Any other little thing you need? Soap—sponge—wash cloth—"

9

"Yeah, soap. Toss it to me. Atta boy. See you in five minutes, Clif."

The five minutes were nearer ten, and then Tom reappeared looking considerably refreshed, and, sketchily swathed in Clif's bath robe, stretched himself on the bed. "You said you had a talk with 'G. G.,' Clif," he prompted. "What did he have to say?"

"Well, for one thing, he said he wanted me to try playing tackle."

"Tackle! Tackle? My sainted Aunt Jerusha! What for?"

"Says we need tackles more than ends. Raiford's not coming back, he says."

"Well, what of it? He wasn't such a much, was he? Think you can do it?"

"I don't know, Tom. I told him I'd have a try at it, of course. I suppose I can learn, eh?"

"Why, yes, you can learn; but, heck, I don't savvy the idea at all! You're a thundering good end, Clif, and you mightn't be a good tackle; not an awfully good one, I mean. You don't suppose 'G. G.' has been exposed to the sun, eh?"

"Well, I don't have to keep on at it if I don't show the goods."

"Well, he said he had been considering it, but he guessed it wouldn't be possible to make you into anything, and so he's going to let you tag along behind the team as usual."

"Is that so? Don't get fresh, young feller. I suppose Joe Whitemill will be back. Of course *he* couldn't be the one to quit school. Just the same, he wasn't going so frightfully well toward the end of last year, and I'm out to beat that guy!"

"I think you will, Tom. By the way, how's your father? I meant to ask before."

"Top-hole, Clif. He's on his way to the coast this minute. He's got some sort of a deal on with some folks out there who make oil; refine it, I mean. If it goes through he will be off to England next month and I suppose I won't see him for a whale of a time. I tried to argue him out of starting in business again. You know he's been out of it ever since the War. But he says we need the money; says having a son is a bit expensive. Heck, I don't cost him much. Still, there'll be college after next year, and college educations do cost, I suppose."

10

"I'll bet it broke your heart to let him make that trip alone," laughed Clif. "Or has the wanderlust left you since you got back from abroad?"

"China? For Pete's sake, why China?"

"Oh, I don't know. Why not China? For one thing, I want to see how they make it."

"Make what?" asked Clif.

"China."

Clif launched himself on the other and several moments of rough-house followed, during which Tom managed to become so involved with the bath robe that he was eventually helpless. Clif applied punishment and resumed his seat, considerably warmed up, while Tom, with disgusted grunts and mutters, untangled himself.

Tom was an extremely good-looking chap, with rather extraordinary gray eyes, hair that came close to the copper tone and a skin that in spite of its warm tan was remarkably clear. His chin was a wee bit aggressive, but it went well with a short, straight nose and a good-tempered mouth. He was a little heavier than Clif, while lacking an inch or so of height; but he invariably carried himself with such military erectness that it would have occurred to none that any advantage of height belonged to his companion. The two had known each other for just a year and in that time had become warm friends. Tom was seventeen years of age, and so was Clif, but Tom would see eighteen some six months before the other.

"You've got a couple of pillows somewhere, haven't you?" he asked.

Tom suddenly sat up with an exclamation of dismay. "Why, heck!" he cried. "I forgot to pack 'em! They're over in 34 and I'll have an awful time making Billy give 'em up."

Clif chuckled. "I'll say you will; and Billy's too big to lick! Never mind, I'm going to buy a couple I saw in the village this noon. Not half bad, although I don't believe the stuff inside them ever grew on a chicken. It felt more like cotton batting."

"What good will your pillows do me?" demanded Tom. "Can't keep shifting 'em from one window to t'other! I'll just have to go over some time when Billy's out of the room and get mine."

"Who's he got in with him this year?" asked Clif.

"Jeff Ogden. And if he gets to sprawling his old carcass on those pillows they won't be anything but pancakes! Say, what time is it?"

Well, it was time to get into old canvas pants and blue jerseys and scuffed shoes and head for the football field, and Tom pulled himself off the bed with a deep sigh of resignation.

CHAPTER III
WATTLES IS WELL

I t wasn't quite so hot as it had been earlier in the day, and there was a perceptible movement of air across the field as Clif and Tom turned the corner of East Hall and made toward the running track and the gridiron enclosed by it. To their right the little pond was very blue, its surface ruffled only slightly by an occasional catspaw. In winter that same surface was scored by the steel runners of speeding skaters, brushed by whizzing pucks, and Clif recalled the fact somewhat incredulously as he fixed longing eyes on the shade of the sloping concrete grand stand ahead.

Presently Mr. Otis called the candidates together and they gathered about the bench and listened, while in the stand behind comparative quiet reigned and the few spectators tried to hear what was being said down there.

"Well," began Mr. Otis conversationally, "here we are again, fellows, at the start of the race. In about five minutes the gun will go off and we'll be on our way. It's a long race, fellows, and a hard one, and some of you are going to get mighty tired of it, I suspect, before you reach the last lap. Some of you, for that matter, probably won't stay in that long. If you don't it'll be your fault, not mine. I'll set the pace, and I'll make it as easy a one as I can for you, but you've got to keep on running and follow me all the way!"

"I thought Wolcott wasn't allowed to do that, sir!" protested Johnny Thayer indignantly. "Any more than we are!"

"She isn't," said the coach dryly. "Officially she hasn't. What she's done is get about fifteen of her last season's men together over at Stillwater Lake for a 'camping party.' The party began a week ago yesterday, as near as I can learn, and there's been a lot more going on than just fishing and swimming!"

"Gosh!" growled the big full back. "I don't think——"

"Shut up, Johnny," said some one. "You're out of order!"

There were chuckles of amusement from the old hands, but some of the new candidates looked a bit uneasy and exchanged doubtful glances.

"By to-morrow I want every one of you to own a copy of the football rules. Manager Owens will supply you, or you can get it in the village. I want you all to read the rules, right through, from beginning to end, and study them until you know thoroughly what they mean. What I don't want you to do is read books on how to play your positions. I don't care who the writer is. The stuff is all right, and I don't care how much you read of it out of season, but in season you'll get your instruction from me and those who assist in the coaching.

"I said that Wolcott is better off than we are for material, and so she is. But that doesn't mean that we can't lick the sawdust out of her in November. It does mean, though, that we've got to work like thunder and realize every minute what we're working for. We're not in bad shape for the season, even if we might be in better. We've won before with less to start on. You've got a corking fine captain to lead you, you've got at least half a dozen veterans to rally to and you've got a coach who, whatever may be said of him, knows a certain amount of football and can get work out of you if any one can!"

Again there was a ripple of amused appreciation from his audience. Mr. Otis's grim mouth didn't relax, however.

"Now, one thing more and I'm through. You're going to work hard and football is going to take up a whole lot of your time, but there's going to be plenty of time left for studies, and any fellow who wants to stay on the squad will have to keep square with the office. I'll be generous with cuts so long as they're necessary, but any one who can't play football and keep up with his studies at the same time will have to quit football. That's all. Let's have some balls, Dan."

Followed an hour of passing and receiving, a little punting and catching and some practicing of starts. There were frequent rests, and they were needed, for the material was soft and the later afternoon, while a slight improvement on the noon hours, was still exhaustingly hot and close. Afterwards, in the gymnasium, all candidates reported to Manager Owens and all went on the scales, Harry New, Guy's first assistant, presiding at the ceremony. Showers felt extremely good to-day, and for once the cold water wasn't cold enough. It was well after five when Clif and Tom went back to the dormitory, stopping, however, on the way to discover that Loring Deane's room in East Hall was still untenanted.

"Bet you the old 'Rolled Rice' cast a shoe," said Tom. "Or maybe it just fell to pieces. That's the trouble with those cheap cars; they're

14

always shaking apart. We'll get dressed and go down and watch for him."

So they walked across to East and along the first floor corridor, past the parlor and the office of Mr. Clendennin, Junior School head, and knocked imperatively at the first door beyond on that side. It was Wattles who opened to them, Wattles looking very, very warm in full attire of black serge. He could never be prevailed on to lay aside his waistcoat, no matter how warm the day might be. Wattles looked askance at negligée, recognized no compromise in the matter of a gentleman's attire.

"Hel-lo, Wattles, old skeezicks!" cried Tom, shaking the attendant's hand warmly and at the same time thumping him cordially on the back. "How are you?"

"Quite well, sir, thanks." Wattles' long and bony countenance relaxed in a restrained smile. "And you, Mr. Tom?"

"Never better, old boy! Hello, there, Loring! Glad to see you again, sonny!"

Clif, too, exchanged handclasps with Wattles and followed Tom inside. "Have a breakdown?" he asked as he greeted Loring.

"Fat? Man alive, I feel as thin as an eel! We've just done an hour's practice on Ye Olde Footballe Fielde. Yes, and worse still, listened to 'G. G.' speechify. Welcome back to the classic shades, Loring. The Triumvirate is again assembled!"

"All for one and one for all!" proclaimed Loring.

"Sit down. Wattles, lift that truck off this chair like a good fellow. That's it. When did you come up, Clif?"

"Got in about ten-forty-five or something. I don't know how you fellows find this weather, but after nearly freezing to death in London for a fortnight it seems like Africa to me!"

"Just comfortable," murmured Tom. "I say, Wattles, don't you find that black clothes attract the flies?" he asked.

Wattles, busily unpacking a wardrobe trunk, looked around a trifle blankly. "Flies, sir? I don't think I ever noticed, Mr. Tom."

"Fancy that!" said Tom. "Fancy not noticing! You see, Wattles, there's something about black dye that flies take to enormously. I'll bet that if you stepped around back and stood outside the kitchen door a few minutes you'd be fairly covered with 'em."

Perhaps I have spent altogether too much time on Wattles, but then he isn't likely to get in the limelight very often, and so we won't begrudge him his moment. On the other hand, I'm not sure that Wattles doesn't deserve all this attention and more, for, even if he was only a paid attendant, a combination of nurse, valet and companion, he was a mighty good one. Had Loring's father possessed many more millions than he did—and he possessed a good many according to public report; too many in the opinion of numerous less fortunate citizens—he could not have secured a more faithful or devoted person than Wattles. Nor a more capable one for the position. Combining the duties already enumerated, even in the interests of so amenable a charge as Loring, was no slight task, and while Wattles doubtless drew down a very generous stipend it didn't begin to pay for all that Wattles gave in return. You see, labor and ability may be purchased, but love and devotion are things that can't be paid for. Not, at least, in any of the dollars that made up Mr. Sanford Deane's fortune.

That doctor, as well as many others who had preceded him at home and abroad, could give you a nice long name for Loring's affliction, but in plain English the trouble was that the bones of his legs below the knees had never hardened as bones should. They were chalky, and, being chalky, weren't to be depended on for the ordinary duties of legs. Some day, said the eminent physician a bit vaguely, Loring would be able to get about like other fellows, but just when that was to be or whether it would involve the use of a pair of crutches, wasn't clear. Meanwhile, save that the wheel chair or Wattles' arms served the purpose of legs, he was a perfectly normal boy, a brilliant student and quite as cheerful, quite as merry and high-spirited as either of the other members of the Triumvirate.

CHAPTER IV
THE FIRST GAME

"**I**'m sorry," said Clif, "that I missed seeing your folks, Loring."

"I know. I tried to get them to stay up for supper, but dad's got some sort of a meeting on for this evening, and so they beat it right back. They're coming up again in a couple of weeks or so."

"That shover will have to do some driving to get back to New York in time for a meeting to-night," observed Tom.

"Oh, it's only about a hundred miles. Of course, Edouard will have to take it slow through some of the towns, but he will make it by eight. There are plenty of stretches where he can do forty-five."

"*Mon cher Edouard*," murmured Tom. "Say, your father doesn't drive the car himself, does he?"

"No, he says it makes him nervous, but the real reason is that he can't smoke comfortably."

"I wish mine didn't," said Clif. "He's a perfectly awful driver, but he doesn't know it. He thinks he's a regular wonder at it, but he's forever getting into jams and busting something. I don't mind a crumpled fender now and then, but I'm always afraid he'll get hurt."

"Oh, he isn't so bad when he has some one with him," replied Clif, "but let him get in the car alone and all rules are off. He drives like the wind, takes blind corners at thirty and on the left of the road and thinks side streets aren't used. Once I asked him why he didn't sound the horn and he had to look all around for it! If he has a puncture he just sits in the car and waits for some one to come along and take a message to a garage. He hasn't the slightest idea what's under the hood of the car or why the thing goes when he puts his foot down on the starter." Clif shook his head gloomily. "We had a chauffeur one year for a couple of months. Then dad fired him because he wouldn't go down Waterman Street, in Providence, fast enough to suit him. Dad was late for the office and the chauffeur shifted to second and there were words!"

"I've reached the conclusion," observed Tom, "that the French are the only folks who really know how to drive a car. Look at those chaps in Paris. Why, heck, it's an art the way they fly around and don't get killed!"

"I believe you're right," said Loring. "A Frenchman seems to have a genius for driving automobiles. They're born artists at it. To watch Edouard take the car down Fifth Avenue is a liberal education. I've never seen him flustered in my life. How about it, Wattles? Have you ever known Edouard to get rattled?"

"Great stuff, Wattles!" Tom applauded. "Wonderful suspense! But what *did* he do? Don't tell me you woke up just then!"

"No, sir." Wattles smiled reminiscently. "The fact is, Mister Tom, I was most fearfully alarmed. I was sitting beside Edouard, sir, and—"

"Wattles, for the love of Mike, get on!" exhorted Loring.

"Yes, sir. I was about to do so. Edouard turned the wheel very suddenly and we shot up on the pavement—that is, the sidewalk—and went around the taxi, sir. Fortunately, the sidewalk was empty."

"I'll say so!" exclaimed Tom. "How fast were you going, do you suppose, Wattles?"

"You're blamed right it did," agreed Tom. "I'll vociferate that, at twenty-five an hour, that was some stunt!"

"And you say that Edouard was a trifle flustered on that occasion?" asked Loring with a chuckle.

"Well, sir, perhaps I shouldn't go that far," replied Wattles cautiously. "He didn't conduct himself in a manner suggesting it, but I did hear him say '*Sacre bleu!*' as he went up on the pave—sidewalk!"

"Imagine a New York taxi driver confining himself to '*Sacre bleu*' in Edouard's place," laughed Clif. "Evidently he's a man of few words and considerable self-restraint."

"Funny," remarked Loring, with a wink at Clif, "that I never heard of that piquant adventure, Wattles."

Again Wattles coughed delicately. "I believe, sir," he replied without turning from his task of arranging the cravats in a drawer, "that the incident was not mentioned."

"Well, all this is mighty interesting," observed Tom, "but something tells me—" and he laid a hand on his belt buckle—"that the supper hour approacheth. What about a game of chess this evening, Loring? I haven't seen a chessboard since last spring."

"All right, Tom," Loring replied. "I'll be ready for you."

18

"Yes, I've got several new ones, Clif," answered Loring. "One of them's on football, too."

"That reading's forbidden us," said Clif virtuously. "Who wrote it?"

"Come on," commanded Tom. "I'm starving. Let's make the most of our opportunities, Clif, before training table starts. See you after supper, Loring. 'All for one and one for all!'"

"'All for one and one for all!'" echoed Loring.

Fortunately for all concerned in the development of the football team, the hot weather disappeared by Thursday. After two sessions of extremely languid practice Mr. Otis hailed the chance to get some real work done, and on that afternoon the dummy was hitched into place and a pleasant half hour was spent in tackling and blocking. Pleasant, that is, from the point of view of the coach. And possibly the stuffed effigy enjoyed it. Those who launched themselves across the freshly spaded pit and clasped the swaying canvas legs soon tired of the entertainment. The weather was seasonable, but it still required but little exertion to bring a copious perspiration, and the soil in the pit tasted no whit better than it had a year ago!

High school made her lone score a few minutes after the third period had begun. An intercepted forward pass gave her a good start, and when, a minute or two later, Couch was neatly boxed, a fleet-footed half skirted Wyndham's right end and went over for a touchdown at the corner of the field. But high school's try-for-point was spoiled by Greene, the blue-stockinged right guard. Just how Greene got through high school's line as speedily as he did was a mystery, but there he was, looming large and forbidding, fairly on the heels of the ball, and the high school kicker hadn't a chance to even swing his leg!

The task of punting was next assigned to Treader, and Treader made a somewhat better job of it. At least he got the ball away, even if it didn't go more than twenty yards! High school tried a fair catch, missed it and chased the ball to the side line. Then, or soon after, it occurred to some one to stop the game.

Tom got a great deal of pleasure reading the inscriptions on the cigar ribbons in moments of relaxation. At such times, luxuriously imposed on the crimson and magenta cushions—one didn't lean against the leather pillow on account of the painting—he placed the Poppidalopous masterpiece against his knees and perused it, turning it around as he proceeded. Since he generally read aloud, this was a form of entertainment enjoyed more by Tom than by Clif. Clif declared that he could stand it better if it wasn't for the constant recurrence of the word "Aurelia." He didn't like "Aurelia" in the first place, he said, and it didn't improve, in his judgment, for being reiterated. He suspected that "Aurelia" was a cheap cigar, possibly a five center, and that Mrs. Poppidalopous had cheated in putting so many "Aurelias" into the pillow cover. They had long and heated arguments on the subject. Tom was certain—or said he was—that the "Aurelia" cigar was a very excellent and high priced article and that Mrs. Poppi—well, Clif knew what he wanted to say!—had so generously included the ribbons solely to enhance the value of the pillow and, as it were, lend it class and distinction. Tom challenged Clif to produce any one who had ever purchased a genuine "Aurelia" for less than thirty-five cents!

"The last time I drank that stuff," replied Clif distastefully, "I nearly passed out. Only had three bottles of it, too. No, sir, no synthetic fruit juice for this affair. We'll have ginger ale, and the best sort, too. And crackers and cheese may be the proper caper in New Jersey, Tom, but where I come from a housewarming calls for real chow."

"Well, what do you call real chow?" asked Tom anxiously.

"Hot dogs and rolls, olives, ginger cookies, bananas and ginger ale," replied Clif triumphantly.

"That what you get at parties in Providence?" inquired the other incredulously. "Heck, that sounds like a village picnic! No—no restraint! No taste! Why—"

"Taste? You're crazy! That stuff's full of taste! We'll have plenty of mustard for the hot dogs, and—or do you prefer sauerkraut?"

"Help!" yelped Tom. "Say, who's going to pay for this banquet? I'm mighty near broke."

"Fifty-fifty," answered Clif. "I'll foot the bill and you come across next pay day with your half. We might leave out the olives, I suppose," he added reflectively. "Lots of fellows don't care to waste time on them."

"Gosh, that's so! Table starts Wednesday, doesn't it? Bananas are scratched, too, Tom!"

CHAPTER V
CLIF MAKES AN ACQUAINTANCE

L ast year Clif had roomed in Number 17 on the floor below with Walter Treat. They had got along exceedingly well together and Clif had a real liking for Walt. So far this term he hadn't seen Walt for more than an instant, and then merely to shake hands hurriedly and exchange greetings. He wondered whether his former roommate resented his leaving him for Tom. Last spring, when he had announced his intention of pairing with Tom in the fall, Walt had been as nice as pie about it, but somehow since coming back Clif had acquired the notion that Walt had felt a trifle hurt and that he wasn't going to be as friendly as before. All along Clif had meant to stop in at Number 17 and make a call, but life had been very busy, and then, too, the suspicion that Walt might not care a great deal about seeing him had made it easy to postpone the visit. Now, however, since Walter Treat's name was down on the list of guests for the housewarming, it was indubitably up to Clif to call and deliver the invitation in person. So on Wednesday, after practice, he parted from Tom in the hall below and made his way to Number 17.

Clif's knock on the portal of Number 17 was answered by a strange voice and he entered to find the well-remembered room in possession of a startlingly large youth who, seated at the study table, was observing him with grave inquiry. This fellow, Clif reflected, was, of course, Walt's new roommate, and, although he didn't know the chap's name, memory connected him with a momentary glimpse of an astoundingly broad pair of shoulders obtained in the corridor of Middle Hall a day or two before. The large chap had a pleasant voice, and Clif found his drawling enunciation and odd accent interesting.

"Walt's out," replied the fellow in reply to Clif's inquiry. "Maybe you can see that for yourself, though. Guess he'll be along in two, three minutes, stranger. Have a seat."

"Sure will." The big chap's sun-burnt and freckled countenance broke into a wide and engaging smile. "You're the Bingham that's on the football team, ain't you? Pleased to meet you. My name's Parks." The speaker arose cumbrously from his seat and held out a broad hand. Accepting it, Clif discovered that Mr. Parks had a mighty grip and that the inside of the hand had something of the quality of a board.

"Thanks," responded Clif, opening and closing his fingers in an effort to restore circulation. "Very glad to know you, Parks, too. Well, I'll drop in again."

"Shucks, better stay and wait for him." Parks seized a chair and swung it around on one leg with a mighty thud. "Sit down and talk a minute, won't you?"

"Well—" began Clif again. Then he found himself in the chair, induced partly by Parks' friendly grin and partly by a big brown hand.

"Can't get folks to talk to me here," proceeded the host, returning to his own seat and lowering himself into it with slow, awkward movements. "Seems like every one's too busy to sit down and pass the time with a fellow. Out where I come from folks is—are more neighborly."

"Where's that?" inquired Clif.

"What?" exclaimed Clif.

"I said Providence was where I live—or did live." Parks looked a bit wistful after the correction.

"Well, I live in Providence, too," laughed Clif. "That's why I was surprised. Providence, Rhode Island, though."

"You don't say? Rhode Island? That's the smallest state there is, ain't it? Course size ain't a heap important, though."

"No, and so I guess your Providence is quite as nice as mine," replied Clif. Parks grinned. Then he chuckled, and when he chuckled he had an odd trick of pressing curved fingers against his generous mouth, as though laughing was an indiscretion. "Shucks, I'd like for you to see my Providence, Bingham. There ain't nothing there but about thirty houses. Wasn't, anyhow. Guess it's built up some now, maybe. Probably you can't see the house no more for the oil rigs."

"Oh, it's oil country, eh?" asked Clif interestedly. "I've always wanted to see an oil field."

"Guess there ain't much to see," said the other gloomily, "but a heap of dirt. Derricks ain't awful pretty, and once those oil fellows get in, a place just goes to pot. I get sort of homesick for Providence now and then, but, shucks, I guess I wouldn't want to go back there if I was to see what it looks like now."

"Are you—I mean are your folks interested in oil wells, Parks?"

"It must be fine," agreed Clif after a moment.

"Well, I don't know. Maybe you wouldn't admire it so much. You got to be born out thataway, I guess. Anyhow, it was a mighty nice ranch until that ornery oil man came along." Parks pulled one big foot across a knee and eased further down in the chair. His face was rather square, and the fading light from the windows behind him left it in a warm shadow that blurred the features. Just then Clif felt embarrassingly alien to the big youth. "That was last spring," Parks went on. "He told pop he figured there was oil on the ranch and wanted to sink a well. Pop told him he'd better figure how to get off the place before he went in for his shotgun. But the fellow come—came back in a little while, and he was a good talker and pop finally said he could go ahead and dig over in a corner of the eighty where the alfalfa was. Pop didn't put much stock in the fellow's talk, you see. Course there'd been oil discovered plenty of places before that, but none of 'em was nigh us. Well, they drilled and first thing we knew there was oil spouting all over the alfalfa field! Plumb ruined the crop before they got the cap on."

"Gosh," said Clif. "That must have been exciting!"

Parks viewed him dubiously. "I don't know. Yes, it was exciting, I guess, but pop wasn't so pleased. We needed that hay, for one thing, and then, of course, a lot more oil fellows came piling in on us with papers all ready to sign. Pop tried to shoo 'em away, but they was like flies—*were* like flies, I mean—round a sugar barrel! You could swat a few, but others would come instead. They were milling around thick pretty soon, and derricks was going up here and there for miles around. Finally Pop seen—saw there wasn't any use trying to farm a piece of land that had oil under it and he give—gave up. Say, it's sort of hard learning to talk grammatical, ain't it? But maybe you was brought up to it." Parks sighed and shook his head. "Me, I'm having one awful time!"

Clif laughed. "I like the way you talk, Parks," he answered. "However, you needn't worry. They'll have you speaking like all the rest of us in a month. Which, to my thinking, will be a shame."

"Yeah? Well, I don't know. Ma's strong for having me talk proper, like eastern folks. That's why I come here. So— Say, I said 'come' instead of 'came' again, didn't I? Shucks, I've got a memory about as long as a piece of wire! Well, let's see. Where was I?"

"You said your father had to give in finally."

The narrator arose, walked to the door and turned the light switch. "Guess all this is sort of tiresome, Bingham. So long since I got a chance to do any talking I don't know when to quit."

"It isn't tiresome a bit," protested Clif. "I want to hear it. But doesn't Walt talk? He used to."

"Yeah, he talks." Parks grinned. "I said *me*."

"Oh," Clif laughed. "You mean Walt wants to do all of it."

"Well, I don't know as I ought to say that exactly. I guess what I mean is that we don't like to talk about the same things. He's a pretty nice fellow, though, ain't he? Well, as I was telling, we hopped a train long in June—"

"But you weren't! You said your father refused to leave."

"Yeah," agreed Parks dryly; "but ma didn't. Ma generally gets her way. So we come—gosh ding it, *came!*—east in June and visited Aunt Lida. Pop was so blame homesick, though, you'd pity him, and it wasn't long before he went off to New York City and got him a job. Course he didn't need it, because—" Parks hesitated and shot a doubtful glance at his audience—"well, you see, with them wells shooting their heads off and pop getting so much on every barrel, it wasn't necessary he should."

"In other words," said Clif, smiling at the other's embarrassment, "you're disgustingly wealthy now!"

Parks grinned apologetically. "That's about it," he acknowledged. "Got more money than we know what to do with. Kind of a shame, too, for we don't need it. Pop gets right worried at times, it piles up on him so. Said the other day he wished the tarnation wells would give out. But they ain't doing it. They're getting worse! Ma, she seems to like being rich. Says she don't care if she never sees Wyoming again, but I guess that's just talk. Still, at that, a woman has a pretty dull time of it on a ranch, and works pretty hard, too. Maybe she's got a good right to like living in a New York hotel for a while."

"You said your father got a job, Parks. What sort of a job was it?"

"Well, he found a man had a harness store over on the east side—or maybe west side—no, east side's right—and he got a job with him. Then, long in August, he bought the man out. Fellow was glad enough to sell, I guess, for the harness business in New York's about as dead as the ice business in Greenland. Pop got stung, I guess, and he's sort of sore about it, too. Don't hardly make his rent, and that's worrying him like anything."

"But if he has so much money already—"

"Yeah, but pop don't like the idea of taking hold of a thing and not making it pay, you see. That's what's eating him. Shucks, seems like he's done more worrying since we left Wyoming than he ever did before, long's I've known him!"

"How long is that?" asked Clif.

"Oh, you'll like it after you've been here a while," Clif assured him. "It's a corking good school."

"Guess I like it all right now," replied Parks reflectively. "Question is, does it like me? I ain't properly broke to harness, Bingham, I guess. Fellows here are sort of—sort of—now what's the word I'm after?—sort of clannish, aren't they?"

"Mm, well, yes, I dare say, Parks. I suppose they are at all schools. But that doesn't mean that you can't join the clan. Fact is, old man, you're just about the sort that goes big with us effete easterners. We get kind of tired of our own sort, you see."

"Yeah? Well, I don't know. Maybe I can horn into the herd after a spell. I'm sure obliged to you for letting me talk to you, Bingham. I was getting scared my tongue would get stiff in the joints from lack of exercise. Say, I don't know what's keeping Walt. He went out more'n an hour ago."

"Never mind," replied Clif, rising. "Just say I was here and that I'll be back this evening some time. I haven't had a talk with him since I got back."

"You and him was together here last year, weren't you?"

"Yes."

The big fellow sighed. "Guess you were more his style. Well, I'll tell him you were asking for him."

"Thanks." Clif lingered, his hand on the knob. Then: "By the way, Parks," he announced, "my roommate and I are having a little shindig next Friday evening. Tom—Tom Kemble—calls it a housewarming. I came to ask Walt to come to it. He may not want to, but, whether he does or doesn't, I wish you'd come, Parks."

"Me?" Parks looked startled. "Shucks, you don't want me to your party, Bingham! I—I wouldn't know what to say!"

"Oh, it isn't a party at all. Just half a dozen—well, eight or nine fellows, you know, and something to eat. About nine o'clock, or as soon as you get through study. We're going to get permits to run the show until ten-thirty. Don't forget, now!"

"Well, I don't know," drawled Parks, shifting his weight to the other foot beside the table. "Maybe if Walt goes, though—"

"Righto! I'm counting on you."

Outside in the corridor Clif had a moment of regret. After all, Parks didn't know any of the others, save Walt, and perhaps he had been silly to ask him. However, it was done.

CHAPTER VI
THE "HOUSEWARMING"

Tom was almost irritable when Clif confessed that he had asked Parks to the party, and Clif's description of the chap didn't seem to reassure him. "Sort of a queer specimen," detailed Clif as he hurriedly prepared for supper. "About two sizes larger than 'Big Bill' Fargo was last year. Has a lot of hair that stands up on top and makes him look taller. Slow moving, like an elephant, and just about as—as ponderous. Not bad looking. Broad across the forehead, an indication of brains unfortunately lacking with you, Tommy. What sort of got me, though, was his—well, kind of helplessness. He's a bit uncouth—no, that isn't just it, either. He reminds you of a piece of homemade furniture; strong and dependable, you know, and not bad to look at, but lacking finish. Rough around the corners. And the grain showing—"

"Oh, shut up," said Tom. "Who cares? What I want to know is—"

"Nice eyes and a big mouth that—"

"—is why we have to be saddled with him? He doesn't know any of the others, does he?"

"You're plumb crazy," said Tom in plaintive disgust. "Oh, all right, only don't expect me to hold his little hand. He's your guest, remember."

"Fair enough! You'll like him, though, when you get to know him. All set? Let's go, then."

Clif didn't have to return to Number 17 that evening to extend an invitation to Walter Treat, for, as luck had it, Walter was in the corridor when Clif and Tom came out from supper and joined them.

"Hello, Tom," he greeted. "How are you?"

"First rate, thanks," replied Tom, shaking hands and viewing the other appraisingly. "How's yourself?"

"Fine, I think. Fact is, I've been on the go so much since I got back that I haven't had time to consider that important question. My roommate said you called, Clif, and left word you wanted to see me. Saw you coming out and thought I'd wait."

"Why, yes." Walt's manner was so cordial that Clif felt vastly relieved and even grateful, and the fact induced an enthusiasm that may have surprised the other. "Tom and I are having a kind of blow-out Friday night in our room, Walt, and we want you to be sure and come. Just a sort of housewarming, as Tom calls it, with six or seven fellows and some eats. How about it?"

"Glad to," answered Walt. "By the way, what's the number?"

Walt smiled. "Did he accept?"

"Well, sort of. Conditionally, as you might say. If you came, he seemed to think he would."

"Really? Well, that's odd. You must have charmed him, Clif. He's the shyest chap for his size and age I ever ran onto. I've tried to pull him about, but he won't stir for me. Did he happen to tell you his name?"

"Yes, Parks."

"I mean his first name. It's Lemueljohn."

"It's *what*?" demanded Clif.

"Lemueljohn," chuckled Walt. "At least that's the way it sounds. Of course, it's really two words."

"Sounds like a breakfast food," commented Tom boredly.

"He explained that he's named after his father and that in order to differentiate, so to speak, he has always been called Lemuel John. But as he says it, you'd swear it was all one name! Well, I'll bring him along if he will come, fellows. Thanks. See you again."

"Lemuel John," muttered Tom, as Walt went on toward the recreation room. "He must be a prize!"

"I've got a heap to learn about playing tackle," answered Clif ruefully. "Much obliged, 'Wink.'"

"That's all right. Glad you aren't peeved at me trying to give you tips. Tackle's new to you, and there's little things you don't catch onto right off, see? Thought I'd just mention it, you know."

"Mighty decent of you," answered Clif. "Especially as we're both after the same job!"

"Wink" shrugged. "I don't expect to make it this year, Clif. You and Weldon have both got the call on me. Still and all, I'll give you a dinged good run for your money!"

"Come a-bustin', old chap! By the way, don't forget the blow-out to-night."

"Not so's you'd notice it! I'll be on hand. As the fellow with the hare lip said: 'Iyawyawyawfluller!'"

"What's it in English?" laughed Clif as the other hurried toward the showers.

"'I'm all of a flutter!'" translated "Wink."

Lemuel John was not the only sizable youth present, for both Desmond and Hanbury approached six feet. Billy was in the first class this year and was certain of the right guard position on the eleven. "Swede" Hanbury—his real name was Joe—would have been the logical first choice for full back if Captain Jeff Ogden hadn't changed from half to full last year. It's a fairly difficult feat to beat the captain out, and Joe was resigned to being a second-string player this season. But, as large as Billy and Joe were, Lemuel John still had it over them for size. He was possibly a half inch taller than Billy, a full inch broader than "Swede" and many pounds heavier than either.

Conversation didn't really flow well until the "eats" had been set out, and, since they had but an hour and twenty-odd minutes at the most for the party, Clif and Tom didn't keep their guests waiting long. Of course the original menu had been painfully cut down. There were no hot dogs, no bananas, no "zippy" cheese. As valuable an article of diet as cheese may be, it doesn't sit on the stomach very quietly when partaken of at around ten o'clock at night. The same may be said of bananas, while as for "wiennies"—well, a certain amount of physical exercise is necessary to subdue those delectable viands. However, if such things were taboo, football training, so far as the diet was concerned, was fairly lenient, and sandwiches of chicken and of minced ham, plenty of ice cream, vanilla wafers and unlimited ginger ale answered very well indeed. The hosts made up in quantity what was lacking in variety, and the guests did full justice to the repast.

It was during a comparative lull in the conversation that Billy Desmond, who had been regarding Lemuel John furtively for some time, inquired: "I haven't seen you out on the field, have I, Parks?"

"I've been there three, four times," answered Lemuel John.

It was Walt who explained. "He thought you were asking if he watched practice, Billy. He doesn't play."

"He doesn't!" Billy stared at Lemuel John in unconcealed amazement. "He looks like he ought to. Haven't you ever played, Parks?"

"No, I never saw much of football until this fall. I saw a game at Cheyenne once, but I didn't understand it very well. It's sort of interesting, ain't it? I guess I saw you playing it one day, didn't I?"

"You might have," replied Billy soberly. "Wink," however, chuckled audibly, and Lemuel John, whose shyness had somewhat diminished with the arrival of food, looked embarrassed and twisted one foot around the leg of his chair until the wood creaked alarmingly. Tom went to his rescue. "Mean to say, Parks, that they haven't been after you?"

"Who's that?" asked the other.

"Well, Guy Owens or some of the football fellows."

"Oh, asking me to learn the game? Yes, a fellow named—named New, I guess, was around bedeviling me the other day. He said he was the manager. He said he'd like for me to play—"

"He's assistant manager," corrected Walt rather unnecessarily.

"Still, he might have called himself manager, at that," laughed Clif. "Steve's feeling his oats a bit this year."

"What did you tell him?" demanded Tom.

"Keno!" exclaimed Loring. "You're mine, Parks!"

"Huh?" Lemuel John faced this new distraction with a blank expression on his big countenance. "What did you say, stranger?"

"I said you were mine," laughed Loring. "If you play chess you're the man I'm looking for. You see, Parks, most of these dubs don't know the game. All they can master is football or baseball or one of those low-brow sports. I suppose they lack the mentality for chess."

Lemuel John's gaze passed leisurely over Loring and came to rest on the rug that covered him from the waist down. "You a crip?" he asked rather gently.

There was the sound of a gasp from some one, and an uncomfortable silence endured for a brief instant. Then Loring answered, smiling: "Yes, something of the sort. I can't use my legs. That's why chess is the most strenuous sport I go in for."

Lemuel John nodded. "Yeah, I see. Well, I'll be glad to play with you any time. I ain't much good at it yet, but I'm learning. I guess it's pretty tough not to be able to walk around." He continued to gaze at Loring, his rather light blue eyes puckered in thought. Then: "You don't look very heavy," he added. "Guess I could tote you easy if there was some place you wanted to go any time."

"Thanks," answered Loring gratefully. "I'll remember that."

"Yeah, I'd be glad to," said Lemuel John.

"Big boob!" murmured Walt in Clif's ear. Clif looked over at Tom, expecting to find that youth signaling "What did I tell you about asking that guy up here?" Instead, though, Tom was regarding Lemuel John rather kindly, and "I'll fetch him over some evening, Loring," he announced. "And I sure hope he licks the stuffing out of you!"

Jeff Adams swung the conversation to football the next moment. "Who's taking the trip to-morrow, Billy?" he asked lazily.

"To Highland? I haven't heard, Jeff. Guy said there'd be about twenty-five of us, though. That lets us all in, I suppose."

"Well, it lets you in," said "Wink," "but it's a dollar to a bean that I don't get there."

"Sure you will," said Tom. "Who's going to keep the water bucket filled?"

"Sit on a tack," responded "Wink" graciously. "And toss me a couple of cookies, while you're up."

"I'm not up," said Tom; "but when hospitality calls I respond with alacrity. Clif, attend to the gentleman's wants."

Clif passed a box of cookies and then busied himself with ginger ale. "Mighty few of the fellows going along, I guess," said "Swede," who, stretched at full length of Clif's bed, accepted a new bottle and tilted it over his mouth. "Too far, probably."

"Too expensive," said Walt. "It's all right for you fellows, making the trip in nice, comfortable automobiles, but the rest of us—"

"Say, we've got the new buses, haven't we?" exclaimed "Wink." "Gee, I hope I get to go!"

"You wouldn't go to a game if it was in the next village, Walt," said Clif. "You've no more patriotism than a worm."

"Patriotism," began Walt indignantly.

"He's going to-morrow," announced Lemuel John calmly. "I told him I'd pay the fares if he would."

There was a gleeful howl at that, through which Walt declared defiantly: "Sure, why not? Think I've got enough coin to go traipsing all over the country? Do you know how much it costs to get to Highland and back?"

"You should worry," chuckled "Swede." "At that, I dare say you'll turn in the expense to *The Lantern*!"

"A fat chance!" said Walt. "Gosh, I even have to buy my own typewriter ribbons!"

"Who's going to win, Billy?" asked Loring.

"Wyndham," replied the right guard.

"I'll bet we don't," said "Wink." "Highland's laying for us this time, Billy."

"Let her lay," retorted Billy untroubledly. "She's beaten already. Know why? Because she's scared of us, 'Wink.' Got so she thinks she always has to lose to us. Psychology, kid."

"Psychology my eye!" said "Wink." "What about last year?"

"We won. Nine to nothing, wasn't it?"

"If," said Billy dryly. "She didn't have. She won't have to-morrow. Or, if she does, then she'll be weak on defense. We'll win, kid. Something like twenty to nothing. Well, allow Highland a field goal, if you like."

"'G. G.'" said Clif, "was pretty doubtful about to-morrow's game a week or so back."

"He has a right to be," declared "Wink." "Billy can talk like that if it gives him any pleasure, but I'm telling you we haven't got the steam to run up any twenty points against Highland. Our back field's as slow as cold molasses!"

"That's right, blame it on the back field," said Tom. "What about a line that can't open a hole for you to squeeze through because they're dead on their feet? That doesn't make any difference, eh?"

"Oh, I'm not saying much for the line, either," answered "Wink." "The truth is that the whole team is just about a week behind. And Highland's been practicing for nearly a month, I'll bet. Maybe we'll beat 'em, but you guys won't be on the long end of any twenty-nothing score!"

"Just so we win," said Clif. "That's all I'm hoping. What I'd like to see is the old team come through the season with a clean slate, fellows."

"Some one kill him while he's happy," suggested Tom. "We've got as much chance of doing that as—as I have to get through left guard to-morrow!"

"I don't see that it's impossible," said Clif earnestly. "Our schedule's no harder than usual and we're well fixed for players this year. I'll bet that if we really set out to do it we could."

"Maybe so, Clif," said "Swede," disposing of his empty bottle by tucking it under the pillow. "Maybe so if Otis would let us. But he won't."

"How do you mean? Why won't he? I said the same thing to him and he talked like he thought it would be fine!"

"Sure enough, but here's the point, young feller, me lad. 'G. G.' won't point for any game but the last one. If we set out to win every contest we might do it. I mean if 'G. G.' set out to do it. But he won't. He will use every game as a step toward Wolcott, not caring much whether we win or lose as long as we're a bit further along. See what I mean, Clif? Take to-morrow's game. If we were to get through the season without a licking we'd have to take the Highland game, of course. That would mean doing a bit of preparation. Learning what Highland has and finding a way to stop it. Going up with a few ground-gaining plays instead of the rag-tag of last year's stuff that we have. Same way with the Jordan game and the Cupples and all the rest of them right through the fall. We'd have to point for each game as it came along and not use it just as a practice stunt to put us in trim for Wolcott. Gosh, I'm dry. Any more of that ginger pop?"

"Just the same," began Clif as he arose to find another bottle.

"Wolcott's our meat," said Jeff. "I don't care how often we get nipped if we can just get our teeth in her when the time comes. What do you say, Deane?"

"I think, as Clif does, that it would be a wonderful stunt to have an undefeated team this year. Wouldn't it look corking in the papers? 'Wyndham School Completes Season Without Defeat!'"

"Yes, it would look mighty nice," agreed Jeff. "But I'd hate to have the team work so hard winning the first seven games that it would lose the last one! I guess I'm with 'G. G.' Point for Wolcott is my motto. Say, for the love of mud, what time is it?"

"Swede" glanced at his watch and rolled off the bed, and the stampede began.

CHAPTER VII
OVER THE CROSSBAR

Thirty boys—there may have been thirty-three or -four—can make quite a good deal of sound if they set out to do it, and so the dark blue's prowess did not go unacclaimed. But Highland opposed over three hundred to Wyndham's handful and the odds were much in her favor. It was evident from the first that the Massachusetts school had set her heart on wiping out old scores this afternoon. The cheering and singing were well organized, and there was an intensity—and something of vindictiveness, too—in the shouts that arose from across the field that told of grim determination. Highland had more to cheer for than the Wyndham devotees had in the first half of the game, for, although there was no scoring by either side, it was Highland who held the upper hand and who twice threatened the opposite goal.

That the home team was farther along in season experience than the visitor was soon apparent. Whether, as "Wink" surmised, Highland had been practicing longer than Wyndham is not known to the narrator, but it did seem that such smooth, even polished playing could never have been developed in twelve days. Highland possessed a valuable asset in a long, rangy left half back who could outpunt Ogden five or six yards every time and, besides, get much better direction than the Wyndham captain. It was Talley's punting that finally yielded Highland's first chance to score.

"*Block that kick! Block that kick!*" chanted Highland.

Well, she couldn't quite do that, but the left side of the Wyndham line did buckle badly and Ogden was hurried by a frantic tackle who somehow leaked past Sproule. He got the ball away, but it slanted to the left, barely topping upstretched arms, and was momentarily lost in the crowd along the Highland side. When it reappeared a heartless referee paced it back close to the twenty-yard line, waved an arm toward the Wyndham goal and announced: "First down! Highland!"

Some three minutes before the first half ended Highland again threatened. Then a brilliant run straight through the whole dark blue's team, by the Highland captain and left half, put the ball down on Wyndham's eighteen, and there is no reason to suppose that a try at a goal from the field would not have scored easily.

34

But Highland had shifted her tactics. A fresh quarter back had recently arrived on the scene and possibly he brought instructions to accept a touchdown or nothing. In any case, the mere three points which would have accrued from sending the pigskin over the crossbar were scorned and Highland set about smashing through the opposing line. That, however, was easier said than done, for, although the small gathering of Wyndham adherents couldn't find much cause for enthusiasm, the Wyndham line was largely composed of veterans, and, if they hadn't found themselves yet, at least they had bulk and strength. Highland used up two downs getting four yards through Smythe, tried a crisscross outside Couch that resulted in the loss of a half a yard and finally, on fourth down, heaved the ball across the line squarely into the hands of Tom Kemble. Gloom descended on the Highland cheerers, but, across the gridiron, a tiny but valiant band of visitors yelled ecstatically.

Lemuel John had been a close and absorbed spectator, and as the two teams walked off the field he turned to Walt and said: "That fellow who was up to the room the other day said it wasn't hard to learn to play football. He said the coach could teach you right quick. Do you think I could learn, Walt?"

Considering that Lemuel John was the host and had expended nearly three dollars for the sake of Walt's companionship, it would have been graceful of the latter had he expressed faith in Lemuel John's ability to imbibe knowledge, but Walt was in no optimistic mood. A ham sandwich which he had eaten hurriedly at a lunch counter was feeling like a lump of lead, the forced march under a hot sun had left him wilted and the conduct of the Wyndham School Football Team had failed to gladden his heart. He observed his companion almost coldly and said briefly: "No, I don't."

His communings—Walt was apparently sunk in a discouraged lethargy and offered no conversation—were here interrupted by a stirring of the fellows about him and by the sudden ending of the singing which had been going on across the field. Over there four boys in white shirts scurried to positions in front of the seats and uttered unintelligible sounds, and marvelously the occupants of the seats comprehended them and responded with a burst of measured cheering. At about the same instant Lemuel John found himself on his feet, following the example set by his neighbors, saying "Rah!" at intervals and then, having indulged himself in one more "Rah!"

35

than the others, shouting "Wyndham! *Wyndham!* WYNDHAM!"
After the final shout he eased himself back to the seat, ran a finger
around the inside of his wilted collar and discovered to his surprise
that the empty gridiron had become again populated and that
hostilities were about to go on.

"What's he think I'm here for, the old robber? If I can't play
tackle better than Longwell I'll eat my pads! That dumbbell
wouldn't say 'boo' if you slapped his face! He's got about as much
fight as a dicky bird! 'G. G.' gives me a sharp pain, if you want to
know it."

"Shut up, you silly coot, or he'll hear you," admonished Clif,
grinning.

"Let him! What do I care? I've got a sight more business playing
tackle than Longwell, and I don't give a whoop who knows it! And
the same thing goes for you. You could do twice as well as that Miss
Nancy."

"Sounds as if you didn't particularly admire Longwell," said Clif.

"I don't. Not as a football player, anyway. What the dickens did
Otis bring me along for if he doesn't let me in? He needn't think it's
any treat to sit and watch this rotten game!"

"He's saving you, 'Wink,'" laughed Clif. "Keeping the best for
the last, you know."

"He is, eh? He's a piece of cheese. Bet you anything you like he'll
let Highland cop the game. He's kept his first string in and he's got
nothing to fall back on if we get in a jam. Coach? Say, that queer
couldn't coach a team of performing seals! Who was it was talking
about us getting through the season without a licking? There's one
coming right now!"

"Oh, no, not as bad as that, 'Wink.' Cheer up and see the old team
march down the field."

"Yeah, look at it march! Sproule got ahead of his interference and
we're set back two yards. A swell march we'll make!"

Nevertheless there was a march, and if it didn't reach Highland's
goal line it got within scoring distance, and if Heard, hurried in
to displace Sproule and kick a goal, had put more force into his
swing there might have been a score then and there. But the ball
fell a few yards short and the advance was turned back. The third
period ended with the pigskin on Wyndham's forty-four yards in
Highland's possession and the score board still unsullied.

Mr. Otis began to use his substitutes in earnest now. "Wink" growlingly pulled off his sweater and relieved Longwell, Ellison went in at center and Hanbury took Captain Ogden's job at full back. Later, one by one, those who had started came out until, with the last quarter half gone, Wyndham presented a substitute team with the single exception of Houston, back at quarter. Clif was one of the last to find employment.

A scoreless tie seemed certain when Clif pulled his head-guard on and took his place in the line. Less than five minutes of time remained—ten-minute periods were being played—and both teams—alike made up almost entirely of substitutes—seemed to have passed the possibility of scoring. Between the thirty-five-yard lines the battle raged, the second-string players eager but generally futile. So soon as either team was pushed back well into its own territory its defense stiffened and the opponent was forced to punt. Forward passes were taboo, it appeared, with both contenders, and probably for the same reason. The chance of a throw being intercepted by the enemy was too great. Yet it was, in the end, a forward pass that decided the contest.

Wyndham asked for time, and, with the frantic shouts of the small but devoted band of rooters almost drowning the opposition cheers, held a conference. Houston, acting captain, hoped only to get the pigskin forward another ten yards, from where, if fortune favored, Whitemill could kick a goal. When the whistle blew again he tried "Swede" on a quick slam at the right of the enemy line, and "Swede" got a scant three yards. On a play that started like the first, "Swede" again thrust at the guard-tackle hole, but this time it was Whitemill who carried and who swung outside of end. But a Highland half back had sensed the deception and stopped Whitemill after a two-yard advance, and it was third down and five to go.

Perhaps the ball knew that time couldn't be called until the play was completed, for surely no pigskin ever took longer to sail twenty yards through almost breathless air! McMurtry had sought to put it high, impressed at the moment of kicking by a sudden realization that the goal was dangerously close, and he succeeded. Up and up went the lazy ball, turning slowly over and over. Clif, watching spellbound, thought it would never start down! But it did at last, and doing so it seemed to be possessed by a strong desire to see what the right-hand post looked like at close quarters! Afterwards McMurtry declared feelingly that that infernal ball had taken ten years off his life and that he wouldn't be surprised to awake in the morning and find that his hair had turned white!

CHAPTER VIII
SLOGANS

Sunday evening the Triumvirate gathered as usual in Loring's room. Tom looked rather disreputable with his left cheekbone a queer mixture of purple and yellow. Clif declared he could also discern tinges of green and pink there, too; but Tom didn't act very elated at the announcement. Instead he fingered the discolored surface gingerly, frowned and remarked with apparent irrelevance: "Wig!"

"Won't do," said Loring. "Middle letter's *E*, I told you."

"*E?* I thought you said *A*."

"Well, you don't spell 'wig' with an *A*, do you?"

"Sure he does," said Clif. "Or an *O*! You don't know Tom's abilities in the spelling line. Why—"

"Shut up," remarked Tom, concentrating frowningly on the problem. "Three letters, you said. Middle one's *A*."

"Oh, give me patience!" sighed Loring. "Here, look for yourself, imbecile! *E! E! E!*"

Tom accepted the book and looked. "Yes, that's right," he announced calmly. "Middle letter's *E*." Clif howled and Loring shook his head sadly. "Might be—'kepi'! Bet you that's it! 'Kepi'! *K, e, p*— Gee, there's too many letters!"

"Well, it says, 'Head covering,'" muttered Tom, "and if it isn't 'hat' or 'cap' or 'wig' what the dickens is it?"

"That's what we're supposed to find out," replied Loring dryly. "What's the matter with your brains, Clif?"

"I never could wrestle with those crazy things," answered Clif. "They give me a headache. Or they would if I'd let them."

"Middle letter's *E*," murmured Tom, a far-away look in his eyes.

"Never mind," consoled Loring. "We'll get some of the others first. Wattles is the humdinger at this game, fellows. We did this other one yesterday afternoon and Wattles spent most of his time trotting back and forth to the library. 'Wattles,' I'd say, 'what are "dried insects" in six letters, beginning with *K* and ending in *S*?' 'I'll find out, sir,' Wattles would say, and off he'd go. At first he used to get as far as Middle and forget what he was going to look up and have to come all the way back again, but after he'd done that a few times he put it down on a slip of paper. And he always got what he went for, too. No cross-word contraption can bite Wattles and live!"

"What *was* the six-letter word meaning fried insects?" inquired Tom interestedly.

"Dried, Tom, not fried. It was—here it is. 'Kermes.' I don't just know how you pronounce it, but—"

"Pshaw," said Tom, "that's not a dried insect, that's a sort of a dance. No, it isn't, either. It's some sort of milk folks drink when they're sick, or something."

"You're thinking of 'kumiss,' Tom. This particular word means an insect that's used to make cochineal of."

"What's cochineal?" asked Tom.

"For Pete's sake," laughed Loring, "don't you know anything at all? Cochineal's a red dye that's used to color things with; like ice cream and candy and—"

"*What!* Mean to say I'm eating dried insects when I have red candy?"

"Well—"

"*Fez!*" exclaimed Clif explosively.

"Huh?" asked Loring. "What did you say?"

"*Fez!*" repeated Clif triumphantly, pointing at the book.

"Fez? By Jove, that's it! Clif, you're a wiz!" Loring seized his pencil. "How did you happen to think of it?"

"I don't know. You said 'red' and it—it just popped into my head." Clif looked as self-conscious and proud as if he had won the Boynton Prize in English! "That's it, eh?"

"Yes. Funny we couldn't think of it!"

"What's it mean?" asked Tom.

"That makes this word 'Mizpah,'" continued Loring unheedingly. "Let's see. Yes, that's right! And this one—"

"What's a mizpah?" asked Tom doggedly.

Later, peace having been restored and the puzzle book laid aside, Loring said: "I've been thinking about something that was discussed in your room the other night, fellows."

"Proud to know," remarked Tom, "that the conversation in our *salon* was worthy a second thought, Mr. Deane."

"You remember some one—wasn't it you, Clif?—said he'd like to see the football team end the season without a beating."

Clif nodded. "Yes, I said it, and got sat on by the crowd."

"Well, I'd like to see it, too," resumed Loring earnestly. "Wouldn't it be possible?"

"You heard what 'Swede' said."

"Yes, but I didn't think so much of it, Clif. No one was suggesting that we make any changes in the—the conduct of affairs. As I understood it, the question was simply whether it couldn't be done under present conditions. I was looking over the scores of last year's games yesterday. We won every one except the Horner game, and usually by a good margin. Highland crowded us a bit, and, of course, the Wolcott game was no cinch."

"Well, eight to three wasn't so worse," protested Tom.

"Why, if that's all you want to know," replied Tom, "I'll answer you, old son. Ever try to say 'Nebuchadnezzar' twenty times?"

"No, and I don't propose to. Talk seriously a minute, Tom."

"I am serious. You asked a question and I'm trying to answer it so you'll understand it."

"What's 'Nebuchadnezzar' got to do with it?"

"Say it twenty times and you'll see."

"Meaning that I can't do it?"

"Meaning that it's extremely unlikely. Go ahead and I'll count."

"Nebuchadnezzar," began Loring.

"One," murmured Tom.

"Nebuchadnezzar, Nebuchadnezzar—" At the fourteenth repetition Loring paused to take a long breath.

"Fourteen," said Tom. "Don't stop!"

"Nebuchadnezzar, Nebuchadnezzar, Nebuchadneber—"

"Whoa! Seventeen, old son. That's not so bad, either."

"He was getting his 'nezzar' a good deal like 'nazzer' along about the twelfth time," chuckled Clif. "Well, what's the moral, Tom?"

"The moral is that it's easy enough to do a thing right ten times, or fifteen times, we'll say; but after that you're going to slip up. I don't know why, but I suppose the well-known law of averages gets in its dirty work."

"Probably," said Loring; "either because you grow careless or because you try so hard not to grow careless that you take your mind off the job. But I see what you mean, Tom. You think that it isn't possible for the team to say 'Nebuchadnezzar' eight times!"

Tom shrugged. "Oh, well, nothing's strictly impossible, they say. I suppose I mean that the chances are all against it."

Loring nodded thoughtfully. "Just the same, it would be worth trying, wouldn't it?"

"Sure! I'd be tickled to death to tell my grandchildren that I played on the famous unbeaten Wyndham Team. *But—*"

"Forget the 'buts' a minute. Just to prove that it isn't impossible, there's Notre Dame."

"Oh, a college! That's different. We were talking about this team. I'll bet you Wyndham never got through a season without a drubbing."

"I'll take the bet," said Loring, his eyes twinkling.

"Huh? Well, when was it?"

"Some time ago, to be sure. Twelve years, to be exact."

"What? Twelve years ago? Heck, were they playing football here as long ago as that?"

"Our young friend is evidently laboring under the delusion that the game was not known here until he joined the team," said Clif.

"I looked it up yesterday," said Loring. "Twelve years ago this fall the Wyndham Football Team, led by one Jacob Glidden, later known to fame as 'Porky' Glidden—"

"*What?* Do you mean that that guy played *here*? Well, what do I know?"

"He was All-American two years," murmured Clif, impressed.

"Well, he took his team through a seven-game schedule and not only wasn't defeated," said Loring, "but played no ties. If that was done twelve years ago, why can't it be done to-day?"

"Football was different then," hazarded Tom.

"What of it? It wasn't any easier for Wyndham, presumably, than for the teams we played. Now see here, Tom. We've started out all right. I mean, we've played two games and won both. We've got six more. As far as we know only one of them's likely to prove dangerous. Only one besides Wolcott, of course. That one's Horner. Horner beat us last year, 14 to 3, and maybe she can do it again. But then maybe she can't. If we make up our minds she can't, it's mighty likely she won't. Suppose we win the first five games of the schedule, fellows, and suppose it's got to be a—an ambition with us to finish without a beating. Don't you believe that every one of you, from Coach Otis down to the greenest sub on the squad, is going to work like the mischief for that game? Don't you think that every fellow in school is going to make the trip over there with the team and pull like the very dickens for a victory?"

"You bet!" said Clif, and Tom nodded.

"Well, then!" said Loring triumphantly.

"Fair enough," agreed Clif. "But here's the idea, Tom, which you seem to miss—"

"I don't miss it at all," said Tom doggedly. "I know what he's getting at—"

"Shut up, you poor fish, and listen. The idea is that if we make up our minds; all of us, players and others, the whole blamed school, to go through this season without getting beaten we've got a lot better chance of doing it than if we weren't—weren't animated by that resolution. And you know that it's the guy who has the most at stake who works hardest. I've said right along—"

"And there's still another thing," interrupted Loring eagerly. "There's the habit of success, Tom. If I succeed to-day in something I've attempted I stand a better chance of success to-morrow. I increase my faith in my ability to do what I set out to do. And every time I succeed that faith gets stronger. Success—"

"Yeah, and then you get a swelled head and blow up!"

"Success breeds success, Tom. Let the team win five straight games this fall and it will believe in itself so thoroughly that you just can't beat it!"

"I won't have to," growled Tom. "It'll beat itself by being overconfident!"

"There's that danger, yes. But it can be guarded against. Now, honestly, isn't it worth trying?"

"Trying? Sure! I'll try! Only, as good as I am, Loring, I can't win all those six games alone."

"No, and that brings me to what I've been waiting to get at, fellows. Why can't we three—the jolly old Triumvirate—start this thing off? Popularize the idea of an undefeated team, I mean. Get the whole school behind the thing. Work up a—a sentiment—"

"Society for Maintaining the Inviolability of the Football Schedule," offered Tom, grinning.

"No, no society, Tom," said Loring earnestly. "It wants to be—to be universal. It must have every fellow in it. It's got to be a great big, enthusiastic determination on the part of the school as a whole.

43

See what I mean? We declare that the team must not be beaten. We keep on declaring it, louder and louder as the season goes on. We—we *believe* in it! We *fight* for it!"

"I see," said Tom, nodding. "'They shall not pass.'"

"That's it!" agreed Loring eagerly. "'They shall not pass!' By Jove, fellows, what a slogan!"

Clif shook his head. "We couldn't use it, Loring. It wouldn't be—wouldn't be decent. What I mean is—"

"I know what you mean. You're right, Clif. It would be sort of like using the start of the Lord's Prayer for a baker's advertisement!"

"Shut up, Tom, you're out of order," commanded Clif sternly.

"Wait a minute," laughed Loring. "What's good all the way, Tom?"

"Biffam's No-Spring Counter Scales," answered Tom, grinning.

"Not so good," said Loring. "But Tom's right about slogans, Clif. They are getting sickening. We ought to have one, but we'll call it something else, as he suggests. We'll call it a rallying cry, or—"

"Don't call it anything," grunted Tom. "What's it going to be?"

"'Win, Wyndham!'" suggested Clif.

"Not bad," said Loring, "only—well, I don't believe we had better attempt too much. I mean we'd better allow for a tie game, you know. Nowadays ties are like the tin can in the well-known conundrum, bound to occur. We're setting out, not to win every game, but to avoid defeat. Got any suggestions, Tom?"

"Sure. 'Don't Give Up the Ship!' 'The Bigger They Are the Harder They Fall!' 'Knock 'Em Down and Throw 'Em Out!'"

"Propaganda," said Tom.

"Exactly, but how shall we prop? I wonder if the best thing wouldn't be to get two or three—more if possible—of the influential fellows with us."

"Here am I," murmured Tom.

"The word was influential, Tom, not inconsequential," said Clif sweetly.

"Ouch! Well, such as which, Loring?"

"Well, Todd Darlington, for one. Seems as if you'd ought to have the first class sponsor the scheme, and Todd's president. And then there's Sam Erlingby, representing the baseball crowd."

"What about Jeff Ogden?" asked Tom.

"I thought of him, and of Owens, too, but don't you think the thing ought to look more as if it was started by the fellows who don't play football? If you see what I mean," added Loring doubtfully.

"Huh, I get you," said Tom. "Want to make it look spontaneous, as it were."

"Not exactly, but rather as if it wasn't a scheme of the football players to work up support."

"How about Walt Treat?" asked Clif. "Walt's on *The Lantern*, you know, and we really ought to have a corking good editorial—"

"Not yet." Loring shook his head. "Later, yes. Anyway, Walt's only an assistant editor, isn't he? Lovell would be the right fellow to go after. But that can wait. Let's get the thing well started first. I'll go after Darlington to-morrow and if he approves—"

"Who cares whether he does or not?" demanded Tom. "We can put it over without that high hat! Say, why not have a meeting and make speeches and—"

"We'll do that, too, Tom," said Loring, "but not just yet. As I see it, we want to be—be insidious—"

"What's insidious?" asked Tom.

"He's at it again!" said Clif indignantly. "Where's the pillow?" At that juncture Wattles appeared, however, a signal that study hour was imminent, and Clif and Tom sped back to West Hall for their books.

CHAPTER IX
"NO DEFEATS!"

They were back in Loring's room after study, and the subject of the former discussion again occupied them. For that matter, it continued to occupy them, with increasing insistence, for many days. The plan appeared to demand a good deal of discussion, an amount rather out of proportion to the progress made. That progress was slow, however, was largely because Loring was the only one of the three with much leisure for action, and, since Loring's trips here and there must be made either in the wheel chair or in Wattles' capable arms, there was a limit to his ability. Fellows had a way of being out of their rooms when Loring arrived, or of not being where rumor had placed them. It required all of Monday afternoon to track Todd Darlington down, and when he was finally brought to bay he proved discouragingly unresponsive to Loring's eloquence.

Loring's acquaintance with the first class president was slight, but he had assimilated the general respect for that youth, and after the interview he found himself wondering if, after all, the project was worth while. Todd had smilingly likened it to winning a foot race by cheering yourself around the course, and the simile had sounded clever and apt. However, as the effects of Todd's personality wore off after Loring had removed himself from Todd's presence, a little later the younger boy began to miss the pertinence of the simile. He hadn't proposed that the football team should cheer itself to victory, but that the school should. Of course, a runner couldn't win a race by shouting all the way, but he might very well win it if the shouting was done by his friends. He began to suspect that Todd had sacrificed sense for the sake of an epigram. By the time supper was over that evening and Clif and Tom had sauntered in he had regained most of his former enthusiasm for the scheme.

"I don't think," he reported, "that we can depend on Todd Darlington for support. He didn't say so, but I fancy he considered me a bit of a nut. He used the word 'childish' once or twice in referring to the plan and the word 'sophomoric' several times. 'Sophomoric' is rather a favorite with Todd."

"He gives me a severe pain, anyhow," muttered Tom.

"Sacred Ibis of the River Nile!" Tom exploded. "How's it any more undignified than cheering at a game? He's crazy!"

"Well, I think I get his notion," said Loring, "even if I can't quite explain it. I fancy it was the idea of the school as a—as a body doing it that galled him. He appeared to think it would be allowable if it was impromptu, extemporaneous, you know, but bad form to go at it deliberately."

"Sounds to me," observed Clif, "as though he were trying to draw a line between amateur and professional encouragement! After all, what we propose to do is only to encourage the team, isn't it?"

"Well, rather more than that, Clif, but 'encourage' is near enough. You see, what we're proposing is not only encouragement for the players but encouragement for the school, too. Not that it matters."

"Neither does that big stiff," said Tom indignantly. "Heck, I'd go ahead with it now if only to show him up!"

"It wouldn't show him up a bit," answered Loring smilingly, "because he didn't say a word against it, Tom."

"Didn't say—" Tom gasped. "You're cuckoo!"

"He really didn't. He criticized it, yes, but he didn't once tell me that he was against it or that it wouldn't do. He didn't even refuse to help, now I come to think of it. The fact is, fellows, Todd Darlington's a wonder."

"So's my grandmother's gray goose!" jeered Tom.

"He is, though. He ought to make a fine politician some day because he can say things without—without saying them! If he was in Congress I'll bet he could vote against a measure and get himself recorded in favor of it!"

"Oh, forget Darlington," said Tom disgustedly. "What's the next thing to do? How about Sam Erlingby?"

"I haven't seen him yet. In fact, Tom, it might be better for you to talk to him. You know him a lot better than I do."

"Yes, but I can't talk to him the way you can. Let Clif do it, if you don't want to. He's got the gift o' the gab."

"All right. No, on second thoughts, I'll do it myself. You fellows have got plenty to do playing football. I guess the publicity stuff, or whatever you want to call it, is up to me. I'll see Erlingby and one or two others to-morrow. At least, I'll go after them. It's plaguey hard to find fellows this weather."

"Sam will be over on the diamond about four," said Clif. "They're having fall practice, you know."

Loring nodded. "That's so. I'll run him down. Any one thought of a six-letter word meaning a rallying cry?"

Every one had, but none of the suggestions met with the approval of the whole and the selection of a slogan was again deferred.

"Great stuff!" applauded Clif. "He's dead right."

"So I think," replied Loring. "But I'm wondering if there isn't this danger, Clif. If the other classes think it's just a Junior stunt they'll simply laugh at it and keep away from it."

"You said a mouthful," declared Tom. "Better not have it look like a kid's party."

"Look here," said Clif, "this thing's got to be launched somehow so that it'll hit the whole school in the face and take 'em by storm."

"Gosh, talk about mixed metaphors!" exclaimed Tom, grinning.

"Never mind the metaphors," laughed Loring. "I believe you're right, Clif. Only, how?"

"Call a meeting, like I suggested before," answered Tom. "You make a speech. Some other guy makes a speech. A lot of us sit on the platform and clap our hands. We plant some fellow in the audience to get up and say he doesn't think it can be done. Clif answers him and tells him where to get off and the crowd cheers. Easy, what?"

"If you say it quick," replied Clif. "Of course, there'll have to be a meeting before long, but I believe we've got to get the fellows in—in a receptive mood first. I mean, we've got to start the fire before we—we pile on the fuel. Meetings don't always act the way you expect them to, I guess."

"All right, but if we don't get started pretty soon," said Tom, "the football season'll be over! Maybe, though, we'll be saving our faces if we don't start until after the Jordan game on Saturday. No one seems to know anything about the Jordan team except where they come from. Me, I don't fancy dark horses. They're likely to kick."

"Oh, I don't believe Jordan's dangerous," answered Clif carelessly. "It's a small school."

"What of it? There's a college down in Kentucky with only about three hundred fellows, and what does its football team do but bite big holes in every other team it runs against? Answer me those! I say, let's let the scheme ride until we've got Jordan out of the way. Maybe after Saturday we won't want to say any more about it!"

"No, sir, it's got to be launched before Saturday," said Clif. "If the Jordan game's going to be a tough one, why, all the more reason for getting the school together for it. We've got to think of some way to spring it, Loring, and—and—"

"Some way to spring it," offered Tom helpfully, "so that it will hit the world in the eye and knock the wind out of it! No, wait, I've got it! Descend upon it like a devastating flood and consume it with the ardor of its—its intensity! Boy, as a metaphor mixer you haven't got a chance with me! Why, I was mixing metaphors for Heinz when you were still in the cradle!"

"Huh," retorted Tom, "if it wasn't for me you two old ravens would dry up and blow away. How about a game of chess, Loring, now that everything's settled so nicely?"

"There isn't time, you chump. By the way, I thought you were going to bring that big fellow down here to see me. What's his name? Trask?"

"Parks? So I was. So I am. I sort of forgot it, though. Bet you he'll lick the tar out of you, too. How are you and Wattles coming out these days?"

"Wattles has had a sort of a slump since we got back and I've been beating him. You see, this law studying of his seems to get most of his leisure thought."

"Is he still at that?" asked Clif.

"Rather! He's reading it wherever he can lay his hands on it, and now Mr. Frost is helping him every evening. I suspect that Wattles is with 'Homer' right now."

"For Pete's sake!" ejaculated Tom. "But I didn't suppose 'Homer' knew law, even if he does lay it down pretty often!"

"Wattles says Mr. Frost studied for the law and then switched to this job. Maybe being assistant to the principal here is a more certain meal ticket than hanging out your shingle as an attorney. Dad says it's going to be very convenient, having a lawyer in the family, because the fellow he employs now is about eighty and has dyspepsia and is likely to cash in any day."

Tom chuckled. "I'd certainly like to be around when Wattles makes his first speech to a jury!"

"Do you suppose he really means to be a lawyer?" asked Clif.

"I'll say he does! Clif, if you or I or Tom studied one half as hard as Wattles does we'd be graduating at Christmas! I'll bet he can recite Coke or Littleton or any of those fellows right through from beginning to end!"

"Who's Coke?" asked Tom.

* * * *

Even the players absorbed the general pessimism. Or most of them did. There were some who remained incredulous and demanded the source of the various rumors. Jeff Ogden, for instance, only grinned when anxious acquaintances sought his opinion of the Jordan team. Or, if pressed sufficiently, he answered: "You know as much as I do, and that's mighty little. Guess we'll scrape through, though." Guy Owens even got impatient and answered shortly when well-meaning friends sorrowfully pointed it out to him that it would have been safer to have given Jordan a later date. Quarter Back Houston frankly laughed in the face of disaster. And there were others who refused to acknowledge defeat in advance; Clif among their number.

Clif's confidence in the local aggregation resulted in the laying of an enormous wager on the outcome of Saturday's game. Tom was the second party in the contract. Tom was certain that Jordan was all that rumor had her, and even a little bit more, and, while he looked forward to the contest with added zest for that very reason, he was emphatic in his assertion that "the old team was sure in for a whale of a trouncing." He grew a trifle impatient with Clif because the latter maintained what he called the "Pollyanna business" and, when argument failed, offered to lay a wager. Tom was among those who believe that an offer to bet is the final convincing argument!

"Oh, I don't want to profit by your ignorance," answered Clif maddeningly. "Keep your money, Thomas, and found an asylum for boneheads."

"If I did you'd be the first inmate! You'd be put in the incurable ward, too, you blithering idiot! Look here, I'll bet you that Jordan licks us, and I'll—"

"How do I know you won't throw the game if I bet all this vast sum with you?" laughed Clif.

"Oh, talk sense," Tom grumbled.

"I am. It's been done before. I've read of several cases where a player has deliberately thrown a game away in order to secure pecuniary profit. So far, Tom, I've found you an upright and honorable gentleman, but how do I know what you'll do when faced by a great temptation? You'd only have to drop a punt or—or set fire to the Jordan goal posts—"

"You make me ill," fumed Tom. "Will you bet or won't you?"

"You insist? Well, what do you want to bet, Tommy? Mind now, there's a hard winter approaching, so don't be reckless."

"I'll bet you the ice-cream cones at Burger's!"

"Ye gods, what an anticlimax!" moaned Clif. "I expected you to say five dollars at the very leastest."

"You didn't. I don't bet for money, and you know it. Make it—make it *two* cones, then!"

Clif managed to shudder quite realistically. "Tom, you'll fill a pauper's grave if you go on the way you've started. Two cones! But all right. Here's my hand on it."

"Mind this, though, Tom. I'll have my eagle eye on you every minute, and if you pull any funny business the bet's off. If you make more than your normal number of fumbles in the game, say three—well, I'll be generous; four—"

"Climb a tree," said Tom. "The last fumble I made was when we played the Rome 'Gladiators,' about 700 B.C."

And then Saturday morning dawned and, just when it was, as you might say, universally conceded that Wyndham couldn't possibly avoid defeat, the school blossomed—yes, really, blossomed is the right word—with blue and white placards bearing the amazing, preposterous inscription:

NO DEFEATS!

CHAPTER X
JUST KITTENS

They were everywhere; flaunting along the dormitory corridors, in the lavatories, on the bulletin boards, spread under window sills, tacked to innumerable trees. You encountered one at every few steps, no matter where you went. They were even to be seen in the classrooms—until the instructors arrived! The school stared and marveled. The absurd things had not been in sight last evening, and now they had fairly taken possession of the buildings and grounds. Breathless Juniors, returning from scouting expeditions afield, reported that the front of the grand stand was almost hidden by the white paper strips with the bold blue lettering. For something like two hours the football game ceased to be the all-absorbing topic. Here was a fine and intriguing mystery! Some one—or, more probably, several some ones—had gone about under cover of midnight darkness and plastered the school from end to end and top to bottom as it had never been plastered before in its history. The difficulties of the undertaking challenged imagination and the thoroughness of its execution appealed to admiration. In brief, Wyndham saw, marveled and applauded, and then asked, quite allowably, "What's it all about?"

"No Defeats!" What kind of defeats? Football? That was absolutely crazy, because one was due in about six hours. Still, crazy or not, it must be football defeats that the paper strips meant, for it wasn't likely that any one—or any number of ones—would go to all that trouble in honor of the debating team! Yes, sir, it meant no defeats on the gridiron! What did you think of that? Cuckoo? Sure, but just the same it was—well, it was rather a magnificent gesture, wasn't it? And some fellows had certainly worked like beavers to put it over! One would certainly like to know who had done it, by gosh!

There were six fellows who could have told, but they didn't. At least, not just then. Perhaps Sherlock Holmes, had he been called in on the case, might have solved the mystery. One can imagine him passing the fellows in review and saying at intervals: "Ah, my dear fellow, you yawn! Your eyes have a heavy look, as though your slumber had been interfered with. Or perhaps you were up a bit late last evening. Watson, you observe, do you not, that the young gentleman seems a trifle done up? Thank you, my dear Watson!"

But Mr. Holmes didn't appear and the identity of the bill posters remained unrevealed for the present.

Fortunately—and designedly—the midnight bill posters had committed no offense against school laws so far as the location of the placards was concerned. They had not defaced school property "by the driving of nails, tacks or patented devices," as the rules had it. The placards had been attached by dabs of paste, readily removable from woodwork, or, as on the trees, secured with toothpicks. Perhaps faculty might have made an issue of the affair had it cared to, but I suspect that faculty was as intrigued as the students by the coup. In any case, it was considered by those who had effected the decorating wise to remain perdue for the time being.

"Well," replied Mr. Bingham evasively, "you see, son, I've been using it a good deal lately—" Then he encountered Clif's compelling stare and ended lamely: "Must be nearly a week ago, Clif."

"Thought so," grunted Clif. "And you've still got that old, worn-out spare on back, haven't you? Dad, I told you you ought to get a new one. That thing wouldn't last twenty miles if you had to use it."

"I've been intending to do that, son, but it's sort of slipped my mind. I'll order a new one first thing Monday morning."

Clif looked as if he had still another matter on his mind, but just then Mr. Otis came down the steps and Clif introduced him to his father. Mr. Bingham was tall and well built, a fine figure of a man in his long motoring coat and cap. He looked almost too youthful to be Clif's father; and sometimes it was Clif's secret notion that he acted too youthful, too! There were, indeed, times when Clif had to supply the dignity for both. Clif considered his father awfully good-looking, which he was, and of late he had begun to fear that, now that he was no longer at home to keep an eye on him, he would go and get married again. Clif's mother had died when he was quite a little kid, but he remembered her very well and was loyal to that memory. He would, he thought, simply hate having a stepmother! To be sure, Mr. Bingham had not so far provided grounds for Clif's uneasiness, but last month, in London, he had certainly taken some watching!

When Mr. Otis had gone on they went upstairs to the room that had been previously engaged by Clif, and Mr. Bingham opened his bag and produced a handsome box of glacé fruits. Clif was extremely fond of that particular confection and there was a strained look in his eyes as he gazed at the box and shook his head. "Gee, dad," he muttered, "I can't eat candy! I'm in training!"

"By Jove, I forgot that! Too bad, son! Well, take it along and give it to some one who can. How are you getting on?"

"Only fair," replied Clif ruefully. "I wish 'G. G.' hadn't switched me from end."

"Hm," said Mr. Bingham dryly. "As a matter of fact, Clif, I meant in your school work."

"Oh, that! Pretty good, sir. Say, wait till I tell you about the stunt we worked last night, dad!" So Mr. Bingham, while he washed and changed into the decorous attire befitting the father of a dignified second classman, was told about the "No Defeats" campaign and the posters, and was led to the window and ordered to lean out and crane his neck until he could see one of the blue-and-white slips adorning a tree at the next corner.

"Very neat," said Mr. Bingham. "But, look here, son, won't the faculty get up on their ear, eh?"

"I should say not!" Mr. Bingham shook his head sadly. "My goodness, what the present generation is coming to I don't know!"

"Shucks," laughed Clif, "that isn't a patch on some of the things you did when you were at school! Guess you've forgot telling me about them, eh?"

"Did I?" murmured dad. "Well, you must allow for exaggeration, Clif. You know how it is when you want to tell a good story. But I say, I've got an idea! Why not get a lot of buttons and wear them? You know, campaign buttons. White, with 'No Defeats' in blue letters. Wouldn't that—"

But Clif was out of his chair and shaking his fists. "Great, dad! How'd you think of it? The very thing! Say, that's simply corking! Look here, sir, could you—"

"I could, son. I know the very place to get them. You leave it to me and I'll attend to it Monday and have them sent to you inside four days. They can do it in that time, as I happen to know." Mr. Bingham took out a little silver-cornered book, detached a tiny pencil from it and looked across. "How many do you want?"

"Pshaw, you'll want more than that. The things get lost. Besides, three hundred won't cost any more, I guess. Dark blue letters, eh?"

"Yes, sir; and big. You know, sort of—sort of startling!"

"Well, I guess you can't get very big letters on a small celluloid button, Clif; but I'll tell them to make them as big as they can."

"Thanks, dad. Say, those buttons will be great, won't they? Gee, I'll bet we're going to put this thing over big!"

"Fine! But can you do it, son? I mean, can you get through without being beaten?"

"I think so," answered Clif hesitantly. "We're sure going to try. Loring thinks that if we can really get the crowd to believing it, we'll do it. Do you, dad?"

"Hm, that's hard to say. There's no doubt that you can do a thing a heap better for thinking you can, though. But you fellows will have to play football, too!"

"Yes, sir, I guess we will." Clif's gravity lightened and he chuckled. "Most of the crowd think we're going to get licked to-day!"

"To-day? How's that?"

Clif shook his head. "I don't just know, sir. Some one started a rumor that Jordan is awfully good and it just kept on getting bigger and bigger. Now most every one believes it, I guess. We're not supposed to have a chance. It—it's sort of funny."

"What do you think?" Mr. Bingham sat down, selected a cigar from a leather case and sighed comfortably.

"I've bet Tom a couple of ice-cream cones that we'll win; but, gosh, when every one else talks defeat you sort of wonder if there isn't something in it!"

"Well, but is this Jordan crowd so good, son?"

"That's the funny part of it, sir. No one seems to know! We can't find any records of theirs. They don't play any of the teams we play. They—they're sort of an unknown quantity."

"The X in your problem, eh? Well, we'll hope for the best. Are you playing this afternoon?"

Clif shook his head sadly. "I'm afraid not. Oh, he may let me in for a while, like he did last week, but Joe Weldon's still got the call for the position. Mr. Otis told me when he first talked about it that if I didn't show the goods he'd put me back at end. I sort of wish he would. I'd be sure of my place then. Tom's got his place cinched all right, and I'd be the same way if 'G. G.' hadn't got this fool notion in his bean."

"But doesn't the fact that he's still using you at tackle indicate that he's pretty well satisfied with what you're doing? Downstairs there he spoke very well of your playing."

"Jeff Adams? He's your captain?"

"No, sir, that's Jeff Ogden. It's the first names that got you mixed. You'll remember Ogden when you see him. He was with us last spring one day. He was our pitching ace, sir. He and Adams are both called Jeff, but Ogden's name is Jeffreys and Adams' is Jefferson. Sounds like a list of the presidents, doesn't it?"

"Hm, reversed, yes. Lunching with me, son?"

"No, sir, I can't. Best I can do is dinner to-morrow. May I bring Tom?"

"Surely, and another chap if you like. How's my friend Walter?"

"Fine, sir. I'll ask him. Gosh, I've got a recitation in six minutes! Come on over with me, dad. I say, you haven't seen our room yet! You wait up there and I'll be through in forty-five minutes. Nothing afterwards until eleven-forty. How'd you like to lunch at school?"

"No, I guess not, thanks," answered Mr. Bingham a trifle grimly. "I tried that once last spring, if you remember, and they put me next to a talkative lady and I nearly starved!"

"Mrs. Flood, sir, the matron," chuckled Clif. "I'll bet you made eyes at her, dad. She's been looking sort of wistful ever since!"

Mr. Bingham reached for Clif's legs with his cane, but the legs whisked themselves out of reach and led the way down the stairs.

Jordan arrived on the scene at a little after one o'clock, almost breathlessly observed by the Wyndham students, nearly a hundred of whom happened—designedly—to be out in front when the big motor bus rolled up the drive and around the corner of East Hall to the gymnasium. That first view of the enemy was slightly disappointing. Dressed in civies, they didn't look nearly so big nor ferocious as report had pictured them. Nor were there very many of them. However, you couldn't tell much about them, as the bus didn't loiter, and street attire may disguise a player considerably. Wyndham decided to reserve judgment.

But some forty minutes later, trotting out on the field in their neat and surprisingly immaculate green and white sweaters and hose, the Jordan heroes were again disappointing. They were not giants after all. They weren't even sizable! Well, there were several quite tall youths in the number, but they were also slim and apparently lacking in muscular development. And they looked awfully young, too; as if seventeen might be the average age. Wyndham, assembled early for the exciting event, stared and stared again, at first in surprise, then in disillusionment. A murmur of something very like chagrin moved across the stand. Wyndham felt cheated!

"Tom!"

"Huh?"

"I'll take a maple walnut!"

Tom only shook his head incredulously.

A few minutes later the game began.

It can be best disposed of in terms of scoring. At the end of the first twelve-minute period the score was Wyndham 9, Jordan 0. At the end of the half it was Wyndham 22, Jordan 0. When the third quarter was over, the dark blue's line-up then consisting almost wholly of substitutes—Clif amongst them—the figures were 29 to 0. When the memorable contest had finally dragged to its end the score stood, Wyndham 36, Jordan 0.

Then Clif hurdled a bench and made the corner of the alley just ahead of a shoe.

CHAPTER XI
LEMUEL JOHN

I t was curious how many fellows were to be found that evening who had expected all along that Wyndham would capture the game. Indeed, it was difficult to discover any one who, no matter what he had predicted, had not secretly known that Jordan couldn't win. A Junior named Seton—prophetic cognomen if you pronounced it with the short E!—was seriously man-handled by exasperated classmates because, having yesterday stoutly maintained that Wyndham would score, he now went about reminding the world of the fact. The monitor to whom the victim made appeal dismissed the case curtly. "Justifiable assault," he called it!

Chance mention of Lemuel John Parks reminded Tom of his promise, and that evening after supper was over he routed Lemuel John out of Number 17 and conducted him down to Loring's room, where Clif and Sam Erlingby were already on hand. Sam was a first class fellow who pitched on the nine and was a general favorite throughout the school. After a few minutes Tom set the small table in front of Loring's chair, placed the chessboard and chessmen on it and ceremoniously escorted a grinning but slightly embarrassed Lemuel John to a seat opposite. Then he said earnestly: "Parks, this fellow beats me at this game too often. I want r-r-revenge, and it's up to you, my friend, to produce it. Something tells me that you can lick the hide off him. Go to it and win the gratitude of—of—"

"Oh, I don't play much of a game," demurred Lemuel John modestly, setting his men. "I guess Deane can beat me, all right."

"That's the wrong thought," Tom protested. "Confidence, Parks, confidence! Summon the will to win, my lad! Remember, my happiness depends on you!"

So Tom sat down, affecting nerve-wracked suspense, and watched. Sam, who didn't understand the game, was politely silent. Clif pulled a book from a shelf and read. But he didn't read long, for very soon there was a triumphant yelp from Tom and that youth was shaking Lemuel John's hand and offering him half his kingdom. And Loring was shaking his head and staring, smiling ruefully, at the board.

"I guess he didn't try very hard," said Lemuel John. "He—"

"Try?" exclaimed Tom. "Try! Man, the perspiration was standing out in drops on his marble dome! Look at that countenance! Does it show utter exhaustion or doesn't it? Thank you, it does!"

"I think you're too good for me, Parks," laughed Loring; "but I'd like to try you again some time. It's mighty interesting, playing with some one whose stuff is new to you. Now Tom, or Wattles, either—"

"Prepare for insults!" hissed Tom dramatically.

"No, I was only going to say that I can generally tell beforehand what your move will be. Parks makes me guess."

"I'll say he does!" Tom showed a disposition to start the hand shaking all over again. "And he makes you guess wrong, too, young Mr. Lasker! Ah, revenge is sweet, *mon cher* Alphonse!"

But Clif fought him off, refusing to be embraced.

"I had a hunch he could," replied Tom. "I sort of like the big queer."

"Yes," agreed Loring thoughtfully. "I wonder if he's a sample of the sort they raise where he comes from. Wisconsin, isn't it?"

"Some place up there," answered Tom vaguely.

"Wyoming," said Clif. "He seems a mighty decent fellow, I say. Too bad he doesn't play football, eh? Look at the shoulders on him!"

"I was wondering about that," said Loring. "Why shouldn't he play, Clif?"

"He should, I suppose. Thing is, he never has, doesn't know how and doesn't want to learn. And, of course, he isn't the sort of fellow they'd be likely to draft. I mean by that he isn't exactly promising. Of course he's built for it, you might say, but he's frightfully awkward and kind of slow. I dare say Steve New was frightfully relieved when Lemuel John refused to have anything to do with his old game."

"He isn't any more awkward than lots of fellows I've seen trying for the team," said Tom. "He really ought to go out, fellows, because they'll be needing some one like him next year. What class is he? Second, eh?"

"Parks ought to be playing with the Scrub right now," said Tom decidedly. "Wonder 'Cocky' doesn't grab him. Bet you he would if he thought of it."

"You know," observed Loring, "I have a sort of theory that the ideal football player, lineman especially, is a lot like Parks in the beginning. I'd like to take him myself and see what I could do with him. I mean, that is, if I were—well, able to get about."

"I'm not sure you couldn't make a player of him as it is, Loring," said Clif. "Of course, he'd have to be willing."

"No, I couldn't do it as things are," answered Loring. "If I were you, Clif, or Tom, I'd like to try it. You see, Parks has a lot to start with; size and weight and strength and the sort of temperament that makes steady players. And he doesn't look as if he ever had an ache or a pain. He's rather awkward and he's easily embarrassed—"

"It's a crowd that makes him that way," interpolated Clif. "There wasn't any embarrassment about him the day I ran in on him in his room."

"I was going to say," continued Loring, "that awkwardness and—and shyness suggest a kind of stupidity in most fellows, but I don't believe Parks is stupid. No fellow who can see the right move in chess as quickly as he can is stupid; not by a long sight!"

"All right," said Tom. "Grant that he's a wonder, Loring, and what about it?"

"Then, if he is, he ought to be trying to learn to play football. We're out to have the team come through without a beating, and it seems to me that we oughtn't to miss a trick, Tom. If we see any way of making success more certain we should take hold."

"Meaning," asked Tom dubiously, "that you think Parks' playing on the Scrub would hold the first team to a clean record?"

"Why not? If Parks turned out to be a good guard or tackle—"

"Too slow for tackle," said Clif.

"I'm not so sure. You'd see a big difference in him after a week's practice. Anyhow, guard or tackle, if he proved good he'd strengthen the second, and the stronger the second is the better the first will be. Because, you know as well as I do, that it's the opposition and experience the big team gets from the Scrub that counts the most. It's the daily battles and not the Saturday scraps that teach the first team fellows what to do and how to do it."

"Think so?" asked Tom. "Well, perhaps you're right. Just the same, I can't see Lemuel John Parks setting the world on fire as a football artist! Why, heck, common sense will tell you that no fellow named Lemuel John could ever win renown!"

"I'm not talking about his winning renown," answered Loring seriously. "When you come to that, how many fellows who play line positions ever do win it? Perhaps one in ten ever sees his name in a paper outside a line-up, Tom. It's you backfield fellows who get the bouquets."

"And us linemen who do the honest-to-gosh work," said Clif.

"Huh! We spend most of our time helping you guys out," replied Tom. "If we weren't right behind you on defense, old timer, you'd lose your jobs. I don't see that you need more than five men on a football team, anyway; a center to put the ball in play and four backs to do the work. The other six are just in the way!"

"In the other team's way, you mean," Clif laughed.

"I really think," said Loring, not to be turned aside by levity, "that it's up to us to persuade Parks to have a go at it."

"Oh, have a heart!" Tom protested. "Let some one else do it. Get Guy on his trail."

"All right, let Owens try him first. If Owens fails we'll get after him."

"I don't believe you'll be able to interest Guy," said Clif. "'G. G.' isn't looking for any more candidates now, and Guy won't bother to find men for 'Cocky's' team. Why not sick 'Cocky' on him?"

"That's the stuff," commended Tom. "Or—hold on; who's captain of that bunch?"

"Warner. Plays left guard," said Clif.

"Hm, I wonder if he'd be keen for another guard!"

"He certainly would," replied Clif stoutly. "I know George Warner. He's a fine, straight chap. I'm going to speak to him about Lemuel John the first thing to-morrow. Only thing is, fellows, it's sort of late in the season to join up."

George Warner, captain of the second team, button-holed by Clif the next morning in the corridor, was interested until Clif had divulged the identity of the tentative candidate. Then Warner grinned. "Why, Clif, I know that fellow. I mean I've seen him around. Couldn't help seeing him very well!"

"Well, what do you say? You really ought to have him, George. He's got the making of a nice player."

"Who said so?" asked Warner incredulously.

"I've heard several fellows say so. Besides, you've only to look at him!"

"I've looked at him and I don't see it," replied the captain, shaking his head. "He's big, all right, and he's built pretty well, but so's an elephant, Clif. You couldn't get that fellow to move out of a walk, I'll bet! Still, if you put it as a favor—"

"Favor be hanged! I'm trying to do you poor nuts a good turn. Parks would make a corking guard, with a bit of training, and you sure need one!"

Warner acknowledged the insult with a wider grin. "All right, old chap. You tell your friend to show up this afternoon in togs and I'll speak to 'Cocky' about him. Maybe we can use him somewhere."

"That's not the idea," replied Clif. "He isn't going to come out just for my telling him to. That's the point. He doesn't want to play—"

"Listen, George, and try to get this, will you?" said Clif patiently. "Parks is good material but he doesn't care a hang about playing on your old outfit. But you need him. Yes, you do, too. A week or so from now you'll be wishing hard you had a couple more big linemen to take the place of the killed and injured. What you've got to do is see him and tell him he's wanted and that it won't do him a mite of good to refuse. He will play if he thinks he has to. Understand now?"

"Sure, I understand," jeered Warner; "but I've got plenty of troubles without hunting them, Clif. *I* don't want the chap!"

"I tell you you do," persisted Clif. "The Scrub needs him. Now don't be an ass, George. Go on and do like I tell you. He rooms with Walt Treat in Number 17, West."

"I know where he rooms," muttered Warner. "He's in my corridor. I ran into him the other morning and nearly dislocated my neck! Oh, all right; but, gosh ding it, Clif, there's not a bit of sense in it. Mr. Babcock will think I'm plumb crazy. And I'll tell you this, too. I'll ask him to play, but I'm hanged if I'll coax him!"

"I don't want you to coax him," replied Clif cheerfully. "Coaxing probably wouldn't fetch him. You've got to threaten him."

"See him to-day, will you, George?" asked Clif.

"Yes, I'll look him up this morning. He's in my Latin class and I guess I can get him there. Listen, Clif, don't make any more weird discoveries, eh? Or, if you do, take 'em on the first!"

Turning from Warner, Clif encountered Todd Darlington on his way to the staircase, and to Clif's surprise Todd stopped. "Say,

Bingham, you're in with Deane on this 'No Defeats' thing, aren't you? I think he mentioned you the other day in connection with the scheme. Well, you've certainly started it nicely. I was surprised, really, because when Deane spoke of it to me I was afraid the fellows would shy away from it. No reason why they should, of course, except that it's just a trifle sensational, if you see what I mean. Then, too, when the team does get licked, and I guess even Deane doesn't really expect it to win every game, it's going to make us all feel a bit foolish, isn't it?"

"I don't think so," answered Clif. "There's no reason why one should feel foolish because one tries a thing and fails. That would keep a lot of us from trying, Darlington."

C lif wasn't able to discover that afternoon whether Lemuel John had been captured by the second team, for he was pretty busy until the second came over for a brief scrimmage and exceedingly busy afterwards. The substitutes opposed the Scrub to-day and Clif played left tackle all through with fair success. He tried to find an opportunity to ask Warner about Lemuel John, but Warner was in the line-up for only a few minutes and the opportunity didn't present. Later, the matter went out of his mind until Loring brought it back that evening.

"He wasn't on the bench with the second when they came across," said Tom. "I guess Warner forgot it."

"More likely he didn't try very hard," said Clif. "I'll drop in on Lemuel John after study and see what happened. I don't suppose it will matter if he learns that we're interested in getting him out."

"Not a bit," said Loring. "If he turned Warner down, Clif, try to get him to come over here with you and we'll have a talk with him. Perhaps, between the three of us, we can get him to change his mind."

"N-no," said Clif awkwardly; "but I've been rather busy, what with one thing and another. Walt off for the evening?"

"Down the hall," said Lemuel John. "He asked me along, but I didn't care about it. I saw you play this afternoon."

"Oh, did you? Er—were you—I mean, you weren't playing yourself, were you?"

"Me?" Lemuel John chuckled. "No, but it's funny you said that, because there was a fellow up here this forenoon asking me if I didn't want to join the second team. Maybe you know him, Warner. He's captain of the second."

"Yes, I know him," said Clif. "Of course you told him you did want to."

"No." Lemuel John shook his head. "I told him it wouldn't be any use."

"Well, I guess he didn't take that for an answer," replied Clif, smiling.

"Why, yes, he did. Why not? Shucks, I couldn't learn football, and I told him so."

"How do you know you couldn't?" Clif asked.

"Walt says so. I asked him one day if he thought I could and he said no pretty emphatic."

Lemuel John consented a trifle doubtfully, wondering what was up. Tom was already on hand when they reached Loring's room, and after a minute of rather perfunctory conversation, Loring turned his chair a trifle, so that he could more directly face Lemuel John, and asked: "You're with us in this 'No Defeats' campaign, I suppose, Parks?"

"Oh, yes."

"Good! Because you can do quite a bit for the cause, I think."

"I can?" Lemuel John smiled incredulously.

"Yes. You see, if the team is to come through the season with a clean record it's got to get plenty of good, hard practice as well as coaching. Well, practice is supplied, as you know, by the Scrub; Mr. Babcock's team. And it follows that the stronger the second is the better practice it can provide for the first. So far I make myself clear, eh?"

"Yes, I see what you mean," answered the other.

"Well, the second can do with more players, Parks. And it occurred to us that you might be just the fellow to help out."

"Shucks, no, Deane! I wouldn't be any good. I've never played a bit."

"That wouldn't matter. Plenty of fellows do their first football playing right here, and make good. You're about the right build for a lineman, Parks; guard, say, or maybe tackle; and personally, as I told these chaps, I believe you could make a corking good one."

"Shucks!" Lemuel John looked about as though he suspected the others of being in league to make fun of him. But the countenances denied it. "I don't believe," he went on doubtfully, "that I've got enough brains. I was looking at a book the other day that explained the rules of football—" he glanced apologetically at Loring—"I couldn't make a blame thing out of them!"

"I'll bet you couldn't!" exclaimed Tom. "I'm supposed to know a little about the game, but I give you my word, Parks, that if I look into the rules book I get all balled up in a minute!"

"About all the average candidate brings to the field with him the first day," continued Loring, "is a healthy body and a normal mind. The rest is provided by the coaches. I'll swear you've got the first requirement, and as for the second—well, it's no secret that lots of fellows in prep school and college who have made big names for themselves as football players would never startle the world with their intellects! I'm not likening you to them, Parks, however. I'm only trying to reassure you, you know. As a matter of fact, any fellow who can play chess as you play it needn't trouble about not having enough brains for football. About seventy-five per cent of football is doing what you're told, which leaves only twenty-five per cent for the exercise of your mentality. You haven't any good reason for not playing, have you? I mean your folks aren't down on it, for instance?"

Lemuel John grinned. "I guess they don't know what it is," he answered.

"Well, I don't see, then, why you don't go out to-morrow and report for the second."

"Oh, shucks, I don't know!" Lemuel John looked frowningly from one to another. "Think they'd want me?"

"Yes. In fact, I'm surprised they haven't grabbed you long ago."

"Why, there was something said about me playing, Deane. And then just to-day a fellow named Warner came to see me. I was telling Bingham about it upstairs a while back. Warner's captain of the second. He said he'd like me to come out and try for the team, but I told him I didn't think I'd better."

"What did he say then?" asked Clif.

"Said maybe I knew best, or something like that."

"The silly coot!" commented Clif disgustedly. "I told him—" Then he caught a cautioning look from Loring and stopped.

"I think you'd enjoy playing football, Parks," said Loring. "Of course it's hard work, but it's fun, too. Maybe you're wondering how I know, since I've never tried it. I do know, though; and Clif and Tom will tell you the same thing."

"Oh, I guess I'd like it," said Lemuel John. "I mean if I could really play the game. I'd sort of hate to go out on that field and make a fool of myself, though."

"Think so? Well, I don't know. I can be pretty dumb sometimes, Bingham."

"At that, you'll have nothing on the rest of 'em," Tom chuckled. "There's a chap on the Scrub named Kinsey—"

"Never mind the scandal, Tom," said Loring. "There's still another thing, Parks, that I haven't mentioned. That's duty. Duty enters into it, too, you know. A fellow who can help the school by playing football or baseball or any other game mustn't pay too much attention to his own wishes. If the school needs his services that ought to be sufficient. Don't you agree with me?"

"Well, I don't know. I mean I suppose you're right, Deane. I never thought about that. You see, fellows, all this is sort of new to me. I'm a tenderfoot here. This kind of a school's considerably different from the school at home. There's a lot of things I ain't onto yet. But I guess you know what you're talking about, all right."

"The gentleman flatters you, Loring," said Tom.

"I wasn't meaning to flatter him," began Lemuel John earnestly. Then he caught the smile on Clif's face and chuckled. "I ain't onto him yet, either," he said, nodding toward Tom. "He's a kind of a funny feller, ain't—isn't he?"

"He's a plain nut," laughed Clif. "Pay no attention to him, Parks. No one else does."

"Don't be in a hurry, Parks. It's still early. Besides, I'd rather have you decide this business before you go. I might as well tell you—" and here Loring flashed that compelling smile of his—"that I've made up my mind you're going to play. That means that if you say no now you'll just have to unsay it later, for I'm a frightfully persistent fellow, Parks, and I'm likely to make life mighty unpleasant for you till you let me have my way."

"Shucks!" Lemuel John laughed amusedly. "I guess if it come—came to a show-down between us two I'd win pretty easy for stubbornness. But, gosh, if you want me to play as bad as you say, why, I'll do it. Guess I'd have decided to do it, anyway. I wish you'd tell me, though, what the—the proceedings are. Do I get me one of those suits they wear first-off, or do I wait and see will it be needed?"

"You wear your togs when you report," said Loring; "but if I were you I wouldn't spend any money just yet. You've got some old togs, haven't you, Tom?"

"Yes, I've got some spare parts," answered Tom dubiously, appraising Lemuel John's frame; "but maybe they won't fit."

"I can help out, too," said Clif. "Tom and I will bring the things down to you on our way to breakfast in the morning. Shoes, though—"

"Yes, I guess I'll have to buy those," said Lemuel John, grinning. "I wear a nine."

"I guess I ain't likely to trouble you fellows any," said the big chap. "Not this year, anyway. I guess I'll be going now. I've got a letter half written to my father and I'd like to tell him about this football business. It might interest him some. He don't have much to interest him where he is."

"Why," asked Loring solicitously, "where is your father, Parks?"

"New York City. It's kind of dull down there for an active man like dad. Good night."

"Good night. Come again without being shanghaied. And don't forget that game of chess you promised. How about—let's see—how about Wednesday night?"

"Well, I don't know," drawled Lemuel John. "Maybe I won't be able to by then. But if I am I'll sure drop around."

"Think he will make the second?" asked Clif when the door had closed behind the visitor.

"I certainly do," answered Loring. "Don't you, Tom?"

"Well," said Tom haltingly, "I don't ... know!"

CHAPTER XIII
THE BOY WITH THE FUNNY CHIN

On Wednesday Lemuel John turned up for the chess game in spite of certain infirmities consequent on two days of unfamiliar and rather strenuous exercise. And once more he won from Loring with comparative ease. He seemed more at ease on this occasion and didn't sit as though he was expecting an alarm of fire and might have to rush for the nearest exit at an instant's notice. And he was decidedly amusing when, subsequent to the chess encounter, he confided the tale of his experiences on the football field. He was so big and capable looking that, when he told in a plaintive drawl of the indignities put on him by the remorseless "Cocky," Tom doubled up and fairly gurgled. On the whole, Lemuel John was a distinct hit that evening, and when he departed he left the Triumvirate sensible of several excellent qualities, not the least of which was his unfailing good humor. Tom came out flat-footed for Lemuel John.

"You're glad *you* thought of it!" exclaimed Clif. "Well, of all the colossal nerve!"

"That's it," Tom complained. "Refuse me credit for everything! Perhaps I didn't actually make the first suggestion, but if I hadn't—er—nurtured the plan it would have fallen flat. I suppose next thing you'll deny I didn't think of that slog—I mean battle cry!"

"No, we give you credit for 'No Defeats,'" laughed Loring. "And, by the way, those buttons ought to be along to-morrow, Clif, oughtn't they?"

They came Friday. Tom voiced disappointment because they were only the size of a nickel, but Clif and Loring pointed out to him that fellows would wear a small button where they would disdain a larger one. "You know, Tom," Clif reminded him sweetly, "this isn't a banquet of the Kiwanis Club." The buttons were of white, with a narrow rim of blue and the words "No Defeats" in the same color. The blue was not exactly the correct Wyndham blue, for the latter was decidedly dark; but that was a detail.

Distribution was effected with little effort. Each of the sponsors in the campaign filled a pocket with them and then pinned one to a lapel. After that all that was necessary was to keep dipping a hand into the pocket until the supply was exhausted and then drop around to Loring's room for more. By bedtime that night every student wore a button.

Wyndham started off with a rush after receiving the kick-off and pushed Tom Kemble over for the first score six minutes later. Sproule missed the try-for-point. The dark blue scored again before the quarter was over when a long forward pass from Hanbury to Drayton covered thirty-four yards, with Drayton's run, and left the pigskin on Cupples' seventeen. There the home team stiffened and when Wyndham had gained but four yards on three attempts, "Swede" retired to the twenty and lifted the ball over from a drop.

Clif started the third period at left tackle and won momentary fame on the third play after Wyndham had possession of the ball. The shift took Drayton to the other end of the line, leaving Clif eligible to take a pass, and Clif took it very nicely, well off to the left of the scrimmage, and sped it down the field for twelve yards and a total of twenty-six. A penalty set the Dark Blue back, however, and in the end Clif's feat went for naught. It wasn't until the last quarter had started that another score was made, and then it was Cupples who made it. Cupples got a back away on a nice around-the-end run, outside Williams, substituting Couch, and the fleet-footed youth reeled off fifty-three yards before he was pulled down from behind. Unable to advance from Wyndham's twelve by attacks at the enemy line, Cupples again tried a placement kick and this time succeeded, leaving the score 9 to 3.

Wyndham went home with a 16-to-3 game dangling at her belt, more than ever convinced that "No Defeats" meant just what it said!

There were, however, some who reflected that 16 to 3 didn't sound quite so pretty as 20 to 0, and who remembered that Wolcott had defeated Cupples two weeks ago by 18 to 0. And when Monday came there were evidences of dissatisfaction on the part of Coach Otis. He tried Craigie at left guard that afternoon and Jeff Adams at left end, and he made brief experiments at other places on the team. And he was decidedly brusque all during practice. In short, the signs indicated that any fellow who cared much for his job had best settle his nose closer to the grindstone and keep his eyes ahead! Those who had played a full two periods on Saturday were exempted from the scrimmage to-day, and the second rode rough shod over the second- and third-string subs, a fact which pleased "G. G." not at all and which led to expressions of opinion not at all flattering to the subs. Tom and Clif, pausing on their way to the showers to hearken, grinned sympathetically and exchanged meaning glances as they went on again.

During practice Loring was seldom dependent on Wattles for conversation, for some one was usually visiting with him down there at the end of the bench: one of the players, or one of the managers, or not infrequently Dan Farrell, the trainer. One of Dan's favorite remarks was that just as soon as Loring got to using crutches he was going to train him for the track. "And, by gorry," Dan would add, "you'll be winning races, too, Mr. Deane, for it's you has the pluck that can't be beat!" Last year the trainer's optimism had been reprimanded smilingly by Loring. "I guess I'll never get to crutches," he had said. But this fall he didn't challenge the hopeful statement. The possibility was not quite as remote as it had been.

"Oh, fine, thanks, sir."

"Well, you look it; what I can see of you! How are those legs coming along, my boy? Any improvement?"

Loring shook his head, still smiling. "Not much, I'm afraid. Wattles thinks he sees an improvement, or says he does; but he's a confounded optimist about other folks' troubles!"

"Well, I hope he's right. What do you say, Wattles?"

Wattles coughed delicately. "There is an improvement, sir. The doctor admits it, too, sir. Mr. Loring is naturally not so capable of appreciating it, Mr. Otis. It is—very gradual; oh, very, sir."

"I'll say it is," laughed Loring. "If you're thinking of holding the quarter back job open for me next season, sir, you'd best not bother."

"Hm. I'd like mighty well to see you in it, Deane." Mr. Otis was plainly sincere, and Loring's cheeks flushed with pleasure behind the barrier of the big fur collar. "What do you think of our outfit this fall, by the way?"

"It looks mighty good to me, Mr. Otis. I guess we've been sort of slow in getting started, but it looks now as if we were headed about right. Don't you think so, sir?"

"Oh, we're better than we were. If we had a few more pounds in the line we'd pass for a fair team."

"Especially on the left side, I guess," said Loring.

71

The coach looked at him quickly and then nodded. "You've got good eyes," he commented dryly. "Yes, we need something better there, but we haven't got it. Well, I never saw a team yet that had an evenly balanced line."

"I've got a fellow coming along," said Loring carelessly, "who may be useful on that side later, Mr. Otis."

"You've—what?" asked the coach, puzzled.

"I said I had a fellow coming along who might work in there, sir. He's just started on the second, but he's promising and I wouldn't be surprised to see him make pretty good. He's built for a guard. Or he might be used at tackle if he could be speeded up a little."

"Who are you talking about?" asked "G. G.," frowning.

"Fellow named Parks. I guess you haven't noticed him. He's still on the bench over there." Loring nodded toward the next gridiron. "He's absolutely green, but he's learning fast, I understand."

Mr. Otis laughed. "Deane, you're a funny chap. You don't expect a man starting in now to play guard on the first team in a fortnight, do you?"

"Well, it is sort of improbable, isn't it?" laughed Loring. "And maybe I'm being a bit optimistic. Just the same I wouldn't be awfully surprised to see Parks get into the Wolcott game. You see, Mr. Otis, he's got just about everything but the know-how, and I'm looking to Mr. Babcock to supply that deficiency."

"Well, I'll give him a welcome when he arrives," said the coach, with a chuckle. "And I've known Babcock to knock the corners off in mighty short time, Deane. But I guess I'd better not count too strongly on this prodigy of yours, eh?"

"No, sir, don't do that," replied Loring. "Better wait another week or so before you begin to build any plays around him. I'll report on him later, sir."

"Just how does he happen to be your discovery?" asked "G. G."

"Oh, he isn't that, exactly. Owens went after him long ago and didn't have any luck. I happened to meet him one night and liked his looks. So we—that is, Tom Kemble and Clif Bingham and I—"

"The Triumvirate?" smiled Mr. Otis.

"Gee, have you heard about that?" Loring asked laughingly. "Well, we got hold of him and persuaded him to join Mr. Babcock's outfit. He didn't want to at first. At least, he did want to, I guess, but he didn't have the nerve. Some one had told him he couldn't learn the game, you see. However, he forgot it and went out, and I hear that he's made a hit with the second team fellows."

"If he turns out to be any good," said Mr. Otis quietly, "I'll have something to say to Owens for missing him!" After a moment of silence he said: "Deane, didn't I hear that you were going to manage the baseball team next spring?"

"Well, I don't think you need worry. I believe you'll be a long way from a 'blah,' as you call it. Fact is, I was just thinking that it would be rather fortunate for me—and the team—if you were football manager!"

"Gosh, Mr. Otis!"

"I mean it." Mr. Otis cast a side glance at Wattles, seemed reassured by that gentleman's apparent concentration on an arching ball, and added with a trace of asperity: "You see, Deane, the difference between you and the average chap who acts as football manager here is that you have everything except the ability to walk and the others have the ability to walk and not much else! Well, I must start things up."

"Mr. Otis, what do you think our chance is of getting through without a licking, sir?" asked Loring quickly.

"What? Oh, that business. Well, frankly, Deane, I think our chance is about one in three."

"Gee," murmured Loring dejectedly. "But we've got through half the schedule, sir."

"Yes, and I'll change that. I'll say one in two. You see, Deane, it's a safe bet that either Horner or Wolcott will get us, if not both of them. This is just between us, old chap, and not for publication."

"You don't really mean that you think Wolcott's going to win this year, sir!"

"Gee," Loring muttered. "'No Defeats!'"

"Well, it's a noble ambition, anyway," replied "G. G.," smiling down reassuredly, "and it's no disgrace to strive for perfection, Deane."

"No, sir," agreed Loring mournfully, "not even if you stub your toe going after it."

Mr. Otis chuckled, nodded and hurried off. Loring looked after him a moment and then said, half to himself, half to Wattles: "Just the same, he may not be right. I still believe we've got a show."

"Oh, absolutely, sir," said Wattles gravely!

A little later Loring said: "Wattles, there's the fellow with the funny chin again. Halfway up the stand, alongside the post."

Wattles looked and assented. "Quite so, Mr. Loring," he answered. "I don't think he's one of our crowd, sir."

"I'm plumb sure he isn't," returned Loring, "and I can't make myself believe that he's one of the town fellows, either. This is about the fourth or fifth time I've seen him, and he looks just as much like something the tide washed in as ever."

"Oh, I'm not talking about his clothes or his manners," said Loring. "But study that face, Wattles. Don't you see that his eyes are too blamed close together and that that funny chin makes him look like a—a camel or something?"

Wattles allowed himself a smile. "I do see the resemblance, Mr. Loring, and that's a fact. A camel, yes, sir. Oh, undoubtedly."

"Yes, and—well, I suppose it's a perfectly asinine idea, Wattles, but the silly coot acts to me as if he were up to something and was afraid some one would get onto him. I tried to catch his eyes the other day and he wouldn't look at me for a half second. If I was a bit better at climbing steps I'd go up there and ask him what he's up to."

"I'd say, sir, that he's just looking on a bit, like the rest of us."

"Hm, yes," said Loring dubiously, "but he watches mighty closely. I've seen him staring so hard you'd think he'd have strabismus. Do I mean strabismus, Wattles?"

"Quite possibly, Mr. Loring. I—er—the word is not—"

"It means cross-eyed or something, and I dare say it doesn't occur in Blackstone."

"No, sir, I don't think it does."

Wattles chuckled politely. "It would be a temptation, sir, and no mistake," he agreed.

"In fact, Wattles, it not only would be, it is! Gee, it must be wonderful to be able to walk up to a guy and punch his face! I sure envy you that, Wattles!"

Wattles coughed deprecatingly, "I'm not sure, Mr. Loring, I hope that if—when you are better you will not attempt anything of that sort," he said earnestly.

"Won't I! Well, no, I won't, Wattles, for the simple and sufficient reason that I'll never get the chance. But if I could—why, listen, old chap. If I could do it I'd walk up there right now and say to that fellow with the trick chin: 'I don't know who you are or what you're up to, but I don't like your looks and so you'd better beat it.' And then, if he didn't beat it, and mighty quick, too, I'd—" Loring smiled down pleasurably at a capable brown fist— "I'd let him have it, Wattles."

Wattles shook his head disapprovingly, but at the same time he turned it toward the stand as though contemplating in fancy a pleasant proceeding. Then he coughed again, rather severely this time, and said: "The young man is scarcely the sort, sir, that one would wish to—er—engage in a bout with, begging your pardon, Mr. Loring."

"Oh, I say, Wattles," laughed the other, "a fellow can't stop to exchange cards, you know, in such an event!"

"N-no, sir, but—er—one wouldn't, I fancy, engage in a difference of opinion with a person one wouldn't have to dinner!"

"Wattles," chuckled Loring affectionately, "you're a delight!"

"Thank you, sir," replied Wattles.

CHAPTER XIV
WATTLES ON THE TRAIL

O n Wednesday Loring didn't attend practice. This was not because of inclement weather, but because a certain very distinguished physician motored up from New York in an impressive car of foreign make, driven by a liveried chauffeur, and spent some thirty minutes with the boy in his professional capacity and something over an hour in unprofessional conversation. When he took his departure at last Wattles accompanied him to the automobile and the two conferred for several minutes more. Perhaps the eminent doctor was kind enough to compliment Wattles on his care of the patient, for Wattles' eyes were shining when he went back up the steps of East Hall. All this is just to explain why it was that when Clif and Tom came into Loring's room after supper that evening Loring was quite unprepared for Clif's appearance.

"Why, what—what—" stammered Loring in evident concern.

"Lemuel John?" echoed Loring. "What about him?"

Clif pointed to a left eye which had the ensanguined appearance of a piece of raw beef. "This," he replied briefly.

"You mean you had a scrap?" exclaimed Loring.

Tom broke in with a chuckle. "I'll say they did," he answered for his chum. "'Cocky' put Lemuel John in at right guard on the second when we started scrimmage. Lemuel John used up Smythe and Weldon in about seven and one-eleventh minutes. Then 'G. G.' called on his reserves. Breeze and Bingham, you know. Great pair, Breeze and Bingham. Lemuel John looked them over and said 'Howdy' and then proceeded to smear 'em."

"Not really!" ejaculated Loring almost joyfully. Clif once more registered reproach. Tom nodded and waved a hand toward Clif.

"See for yourself. Exhibit one. The other exhibit doesn't show his wounds on the surface so much but, believe me, he's got hurt feelings!"

"But—but Lemuel John didn't—didn't *hit* you, Clif!"

"Passing by!" jeered Tom. "You were just aching for trouble, and you sure got it!"

"I think it was Lemuel John's knee that hit me," said Clif. "I remember that he towered above me some nineteen or twenty feet for a moment, and I'm sure it couldn't have been his elbow."

"You mean that you were down?" asked Loring interestedly.

"Down? By no means. I was standing on my feet. Anyway, some one's feet. Then the cyclone passed."

"Did you hold them?" Loring's voice was eager.

"Hold who?" inquired Clif.

"Why, the second!"

"Oh! Yes, we held the second. Most of them, that is. The one we didn't hold was Lemuel John. Fact is, we didn't hold Converse, either; but that wasn't our fault. We might have stopped him only he got right behind Lemuel John and no one could see him, of course. Not until he was on top of the goal line, anyway. You know there ought to be a rule against a player hiding himself like that. It isn't sporting."

"Good, was he?" asked Loring eagerly.

"Good? No, as a player he was rotten. He broke all the commandments. He got out of position, he charged standing up, he—he—"

"But he got through," chuckled Loring.

"Oh, yes, he got through. He's a rotten football player, but he's a whale of a battering-ram. Boy, let me tell you something. When Lemuel John learns what a football is for and what the white lines that they paint on the grass mean and a few little things like that, and when he remembers to play low and start with the ball, he's going to be some warm baby! I had a hunch right along that he had the stuff in him. You fellows wouldn't believe me, but—"

A howl went up from the others. "Yes, you did!" scoffed Clif. "You were the one who couldn't see him with a spyglass!"

"What do you mean, spyglass?" asked Tom, grinning. "No one offered me any spyglass. I just had a feeling—"

"Is Lemuel John really as bad as Tom says, Clif?" Loring interrupted.

"Oh, pretty nearly. Why not? He hasn't been with the Scrub more than a week, has he? He's sort of roughhewn just now, but I know 'Cocky' well enough to feel pretty certain that Lemuel John will have the corners all chipped off neatly before the season's over."

"Funny Mr. Babcock let him play so soon," mused Loring.

"Not so very funny," answered Tom. "Their regular right guard had a cut to-day and the next best bet got a bum knee yesterday.

It was Lemuel John or a third sub, I guess, and 'Cocky' chose Lemuel."

Loring smiled in a thoroughly pleased fashion. "Only yesterday," he said, "I told Mr. Otis about him. Of course I was kind of joshing, but I said I had a guard coming along who might fit in nicely before the season was over."

"*You* had! Where do you get that 'you' stuff?" Tom demanded. "Who was it thought of Lemuel John as a football player in the first place?"

"Well, it wasn't you," laughed Loring. "However, I don't claim all the credit. I didn't yesterday. I told 'G. G.' that we'd all been working on Lemuel John. Gosh, but wouldn't it be corking if he really did make the team?"

"The first, you mean?" Clif asked. "Not likely, I guess. Just the same, I wish he would, and I wish 'G. G.' would play him at left guard. I'd sure like to rub elbows with Lemuel John!"

"I should think you'd done enough of it," chuckled Tom.

"I told you it wasn't his elbow," replied Clif with dignity. "It was his knee. Or maybe he just kicked me. Anyway, he was terribly concerned afterwards and said, 'I guess I'll have to be careful and not play so rough, Bingham!' I said, 'You play as rough as you like. It won't be anything in my life, Parks, because the next time I see you making up your mind to come my way I'm not going to be there!'"

Wyndham had no difficulty with Minster High School on the following Saturday, meeting the opponent on Wyndham Field and administering a neat drubbing. The final score of 24 to 3 practically duplicated last year's victory. The home team did not, perhaps, deserve all the glory the figures indicated, for Minster was not a strong team. Still, the Dark Blue showed an improvement over last Saturday and put up a firm defense against any attack the visitors showed; and they tried about every ruse known to the game. Wyndham played through without the services of "Punk" Drayton, left end, and Captain Ogden, full back. Drayton had developed a mild case of tonsilitis and Jeff's ankle was still weak. However, Adams, who took "Punk's" place, and "Swede" Hanbury, who substituted for Ogden, were well able to look after their jobs. On the whole, Wyndham was fairly well satisfied with herself that Saturday evening and those who, while flaunting "No Defeats!"

buttons, had secretly doubted the ability of the team to come through with a whole skin, now took heart. What Coach Otis thought about the game or the prospects of the team was not known. The coach didn't confide his opinions very often.

Two afternoons later Loring once more drew Wattles' attention to the youth with the funny chin. "There's the Camel again," he said. "I do wish you'd go up there in the stand and ask him what he's doing. He's got conspirator written all over that trick countenance of his, Wattles."

Wattles looked. "Yes, sir," he answered, "but I hardly think, if you'll pardon me, Mr. Loring, that I would be—er—justified in asking the young man such a question."

Clif was generally believed to have deposed Weldon at left tackle now. At all events, he was being used much more than Weldon in that position and was gradually shaping into a brilliant performer on offense. In defense he was not quite so good, but neither Smythe nor Breeze, alternate incumbents of the next position toward center, was showing up well, and a weak guard may easily bring discredit on his tackle. Tom was going finely of late. Indeed, with the exception of Captain Jeff himself—and Jeff's style was too different to invite comparison—Tom was showing up as the cleverest back on the squad. He had developed a speed in starting that he had lacked last season, a speed that was adding a yard or more to every effort. And he was winning praise, too, as a unit of the secondary defense, making his tackles hard and seldom missing his man. Loring was glad that the other members of the Triumvirate were doing so well. Next to playing himself, the thing that gave him the most pleasure was witnessing the success of Clif and Tom.

A few minutes before the end of the scrimmage Loring turned to Wattles and said: "I'd like to go over to the village and get a book at Leeson's, Wattles. There's time enough, I guess."

"Leeson's is just across, sir," said Wattles.

"I know, but I feel like taking some exercise." That was, of course, Loring's joke, since the exercise fell to Wattles. "Isn't that the Camel ahead there, Wattles?"

"Yes, sir, he just passed."

"You might sort of keep him in sight then. I'm rather curious to know where he's going."

Wattles had a soul for intrigue and adventure, although the fact would not have been suspected, and he perked up at once. "Very good, Mr. Loring," he replied with relish. "He seems to be in a bit of a hurry."

"Yes, doesn't he? Well, carry on."

So Wattles carried on for two blocks further. Then the boy with the funny chin turned abruptly to the left down a side street that, as Loring knew, was lamentably ill-paved. "Leave me here, Wattles," he said, "and beat it! See where he goes to. Don't lose him, Old Sleuth!"

"A car, eh? Which way did he go? Was he alone?"

"Alone, sir, yes. He went east." Wattles waved a hand.

"East? Where was the car?"

"About halfway along the block, in front of a sort of shed, Mr. Loring. A stable, perhaps. There's a carpenter's sign on it. He got in and went right on down Pierson Street."

"But Pierson Street doesn't lead anywhere," Loring protested. "We were on the other end of it last spring."

"It goes as far as the road where the stone machine is, sir."

"Stone machine? What— Oh, the rock crusher! Of course! And that leads over that way to Stoddard—no, Elm Street."

"To Stoddard, too, sir. I believe it crosses Elm."

"And Stoddard Street goes over to the old turnpike!"

"Yes, sir."

"And the old turnpike— Gee, I wish I had a map!"

"They have them at Leeson's, Mr. Loring."

"Right you are, Wattles! On to Leeson's."

A few minutes later, a road map spread across his knees, Loring exclaimed in triumph. "Just as I thought, Wattles! That road hits the state road about four miles north of town!"

"Indeed, sir?" Wattles commented.

"Yes! And don't you see what that means?"

Wattles' cough was deprecatory. "I'm afraid I don't, sir."

"Why, think, man! Where does the state road go from here?"

"I believe it goes to Canaan, sir, and then—"

"Canaan, my eye! Before Canaan, I mean?"

"Before Canaan? Why, to be sure, sir! Cotterville!"

"Cotterville, Wattles! And I'll bet you that chap is on his way back to Wolcott right this minute!"

They talked it over that evening in Loring's room. Since Lemuel John was on hand for a game of chess he was made a party to the conference, but his verbal contributions were few. The Triumvirate was unanimous as to two things. These were, first, that the Camel, as they called the unknown youth for want of a better appellation, was attending Wyndham practices for the purpose of obtaining information which, passed on to the Wolcott football team, might prove of aid to the latter along about the twenty-second of the month; and, second, that such espionage was unsportsmanlike and deserving of severe condemnation. Of course, they didn't put it just like that, but that's what they meant. I have used my own phraseology rather than theirs that the gentle reader may be spared the shock of certain uncouth expressions.

Lemuel John made his first suggestion of the evening. "Guess the best way to do would be to follow him and see where he goes to," he drawled. "If you nabbed him and asked questions he might lie."

"Might?" said Clif. "Would, you mean! Well, maybe you're right, Tom. Only, if we find that the Camel really is spying here and tipping off the Wolcott football crowd, I say we've got to tell Mr. Otis."

"He said it was too dirty to read," said Loring. "Besides, it isn't likely the fellow owns the car. He probably rents it. Wattles says it was just a rattle-trap, anyway."

"Say, how about Wattles?" asked Clif. "Couldn't he follow the fellow and see where he goes?"

"It ought to be one of us," answered Loring. "Of course, it can't be me. I'll tell you. Clif has a driver's license, and can drive, too; which isn't always the case! If he could get hold of a car—"

"But I couldn't get away from the field in time," Clif objected.

"Wait a sec. Where's that map I brought home? Thanks, Tom. Now look here, fellows. Gather around. Here's where he had the car this afternoon. It isn't likely that he leaves it the same place every time he comes over here, but it's safe to say he parks it far enough from the school to avoid suspicion. Anyway, what he probably does do when he starts back is to head over to this road here. What's the name of it? Or hasn't it got any—"

"Treadwell Street," said Clif, laying a finger on the map.

"Painter's colic," suggested the irrepressible Tom.

"But wouldn't he recognize me?" asked Clif doubtfully.

"I don't think so. Not if you were in street clothes. And you could pull your cap down pretty well and sort of keep your head turned."

"'Hink' Connell's got a false mustache," said Tom, chuckling. "It's red, but—"

"Cut out the comedy," said Loring. "Let's get this thing fixed up somehow before the gong rings. Hang it, if you fellows can't take hold of it I'll trail him myself, in this chair, with Wattles chauffeuring!"

"I'm ready to try it," protested Clif. "But I don't see how I can get away over there by the time the Camel does. I've got to get a shower, change my street clothes, beat it across to the corner—"

"I dare say he would, but what'll I tell him? And here's another thing. It'll be an hour's run to Cotterville and an hour's run back. That means that I'll miss supper, probably. Besides, won't faculty kick if they find out?"

Loring questioned Tom with his eyes and Tom shook his head. "Search me," he said. "A fellow's at liberty to cut a meal if he wants to, but I'm not sure he's supposed to be joy riding when he does it."

"I don't think the rules say anything about being outside the grounds at supper time," said Loring.

"Maybe not," remarked Clif pessimistically, "but that wouldn't mean a thing if they didn't like it. They'd make a rule."

"I'd do the job if I could drive a flivver," said Lemuel John.

"So would I," said Loring. "Seems to me, Clif, you can think up more objections—"

"Oh, shut up! All right, I'll do it. I'll get that trick flivver we went out to the boat races in last spring. I guess he will let me have it if it's still alive. But, listen, wouldn't it be a sell if the Camel didn't turn up to-morrow?"

"That's so," said Loring. "And I don't believe he does come every day. At least, I haven't noticed him more than two or three times a week, I suppose. That's a complication, isn't it?"

Clif nodded. "All right," he agreed. "I've got to own up, though, that I haven't got much enthusiasm for the business. I have a hunch that we're going to fall down on it somewhere."

"Well, we can try," said Loring. "If we can't make it go the first time we can try again, I guess."

"What! Now look here! I'm not going to—to spend the rest of the month doing this Paul Revere stunt! I'll try it once, but after that it's some one else's turn."

"Don't be a piker," said Tom. "You're doing it for the dear old school, aren't you? And the dear old team? Really, Clif, you're not showing the proper spirit!"

"I'll show you a punch in the jaw," growled Clif. However, he didn't look as if he quite meant it, and Tom failed to show apprehension. The return of Wattles from the West Hall library presaged the gong, and the visitors arose to depart.

"Sorry about our game, Parks," said Loring.

"Oh, that's all right," answered the big chap. "This other thing's been right interesting."

"Well—oh, by the way, you'll keep it under your hat, eh?"

"Eh?" asked Lemuel John. "Oh! Sure, don't you worry. I'll keep the old trap shut tight, Deane."

Wednesday started in with a drizzle that persisted until nearly noon. However, the gridiron, although moist and a bit slippery, was usable by three-thirty and the sun was out to do its bit. Loring didn't pay his call on the Scrub that afternoon, but followed his custom of spending practice time at the end of the first team bench. Coach Otis looked more than usually grim to-day, and those who were well acquainted with his moods predicted a strenuous afternoon. With the Horner Academy game coming in three days it doubtless behooved the coach to make the most of his opportunities to-day and to-morrow. Horner was a much respected opponent. She had a disagreeable habit of beating the Dark Blue about every other year on an average, and, although she had performed that feat last fall and it might well be considered Wyndham's turn to conquer, there was a feeling that Saturday's game might prove the hardest encounter of the season and even put an end to the prevalence of those blue-and-white buttons. The fact that this year's game was to be played at Horner had a bearing on the outcome, too, for Horner was a long railroad journey away and the team had to start before seven in the morning in order to reach the New York village in time for luncheon. Such a trip is more or less of a handicap to the team that makes it, and there were plenty of doubting Thomases around Wyndham just now.

Meanwhile Loring had been on the lookout for the youth with the funny chin. The Camel, however, was not in the stand and Loring concluded by the time that the audience dribbled back to the seats that he was not coming to-day. Clif and Tom came over for a whispered conference and Loring reported the Camel's absence. Clif looked relieved, Tom disappointed. Then, just as the two players were turning away, Wattles leaned forward over Loring's chair.

"Beg pardon, sir," said Wattles in the proper tones for a conspirator, "but the—er—the young man's there now."

"Don't all look together," Loring warned. "Where is he, Wattles?"

"In the further section, sir. Fourth row from the top and next to the post."

"Right-o!" whispered Loring. "See him, Clif? It's all right; he isn't looking this way."

"So that's the Camel," murmured Clif. "Well, hanged if he doesn't look like one! What's the matter with his chin, anyhow? Looks as if it was made of putty. See him, Tom?"

"You can't tell," said Clif. "Folks aren't always as foolish as they look, Thomas. You ought to know that."

"Hey, wait a minute, wait a minute! What's that mean, eh? I never said you looked foolish, no matter what I've thought, Clif. If—"

"Think you'll know him when you see him in the car?" interrupted Loring.

"Yes, unless he hides that chin," chuckled Clif. "All right, fellows, Paul Revere rides at five o'clock!"

"'One if by land and two if by sea,'" murmured Tom. "Summon the chariot, Wattles."

"Get a good five minutes start of him, Clif," Loring advised. "Maybe you can be taken sick or something, eh?"

"I'll fix it," answered Clif confidently. "You look after the flivver. Tell him to have it down there by the end of those poplars at ten minutes to five with the engine running, Wattles."

"Very good, Mr. Clifton," replied Wattles quite animatedly. "The car will be there, sir."

Mr. Otis' voice summoned the players from the bench and Clif and Tom hurried off. Loring turned to Wattles.

"On your way, old chap," he said. "I'll wait here for you, so don't hurry. Only be sure that fellow understands what he's to do, Wattles. Clif's explained it all to him once, but he's a sort of a dumb goof and you'd better go over it again."

"Oh, I'll make it quite clear to him, sir," said Wattles.

Whereupon, having set his black derby carefully in place and buttoned his coat, he made off with unhurried dignity.

CHAPTER XVI
RUN TO EARTH

It was early dusk when Clif pulled up at the side of the road, shut off his engine and descended from the shabby flivver. There was still a dull glow in the western sky, but it was fading fast and the shadows were deepening. Although he had left the field before the end of practice and changed from football togs to his present regalia of trousers and sweater and cap in something approaching record time, he was still in doubt as to whether he had reached the turnpike ahead of his quarry. He had made the little car hustle, and it didn't seem possible that he had arrived too late, yet, if he hadn't, where was the Camel? Clif looked back along the road, but it was empty and silent. He sat down on the running board and thought rather sadly of supper. He was already hungry enough to eat an ox, he assured himself, and goodness only knew what his condition would be by the time he saw the present adventure to its end and got back to school! And when he did get back it would probably be too late for anything to eat! He began to hope that the Camel had eluded him, in which case, after waiting where he was long enough to satisfy himself on that point, he could run the flivver back to the village and return to school in plenty of time to—

These pleasant reflections were suddenly disturbed. Far back on the narrow road he had traveled from the direction of the school two weak, lemon-yellowish points of light appeared in the purple twilight. Clif looked, sighed and arose. When the Camel went by he was to pretend to be puzzling over a balky engine. He lifted the hood and assumed the familiar attitude of the stalled motorist, in spite of the fact that, had there been anything wrong with the engine, he wouldn't have been able to find the trouble by peering into that dark and smelly cavern. The sound of the approaching car grew louder and its lights played wanly against the bare trees beyond Clif's silent chariot. Then, with a squeaking of springs and a rattle and hum the oncoming car slowed slightly for the corner, slewed to the left and bounded on again.

It had been planned that he was to identify the boy with the funny chin as he went past at the corner back there; and do it without allowing the recognition to be mutual. But, even if he had looked—and he had purposely not looked for fear that the Camel might take alarm—it would have been impossible to identify any one in the half dark. So now it amounted to this: Clif was chasing some one who might or might not be the person he had set out to chase! At considerable risk of leaving the turnpike, none too wide at any point in its leisurely meanderings, he stretched his head around the side of the car and looked back. There was no one behind; or, at least, no one within sight. Oh, that just had to be the Camel ahead there! Nevertheless doubt continued to disturb him.

He continued, however, maintaining a demure twenty-mile gait, for another half-mile or so. Then the turnpike merged into the wider ribbon of the state road and the hard, smooth paving glistened under the lights of the car. Clif stopped short and made pretense of looking for signs. There were plenty of them, although as usual they were more concerned with the merits of suspenders, self-rising flour, automobile oil and other merchandise than with the destination of the roads. But the ruse worked, for the Camel's flivver passed again and, as though the driver had decided that his neighbor on the road was a harmless tourist, took up its former headlong flight. Clif grinned and followed.

Clif believed now that the Camel was aware that he was being trailed. Otherwise, or so it seemed to the pursuer, he wouldn't have driven so recklessly. After all, if the Camel had only to travel as far as Cotterville he had plenty of time to reach that town before six o'clock, and he needn't have taken such chances as he had. Clif recalled Loomis as being a place of some size, with a bridge across a rocky river bed—occasionally showing water—a factory of some sort that stretched for a good block along the main road and numerous small alleylike streets leading left and right. It wouldn't be a difficult feat for the Camel to turn into one of those streets and give him the shake, Clif reflected; especially if the Camel knew the village. So, when the Camel reduced his forty-mile speed to something about thirty, Clif didn't follow his example at once. He waited until scarcely more than a dozen yards intervened between the two cars, and presently he was glad he had done so. A few stores, still open for business, a fire house, a white Town Hall went past on the left and the factory loomed ahead, its hundreds of windows dark. Just beyond was the bridge, in fair sight under the light of an arc lamp. But suddenly the flivver in the lead swerved sharply to the right and was gone!

Puzzled for an instant, Clif sent his complaining chariot forward at its best pace. But then the explanation came to him. The Camel had not left the state road, but had doused his lights! Well, if he wanted to take the risk, all right; fortunately, Clif didn't have to. And perhaps the risk wasn't so great, after all, for the road passed through open country here and the starlight was not filtered through the trees as it had been further back. In any case, the Camel kept his pace, and Clif, even with the aid of his lights, had to hustle to keep the dim form of the other car in sight. In such manner they passed a little hamlet where, beyond an uncurtained casement, Clif saw a tall, thin man lifting food to his mouth. It was the briefest sort of a vision, but it was painfully clear, and right then Clif's flivver almost went into a telephone pole! Recovering control, he wondered sadly if they would have given him food after dragging his body from the wreck!

Mr. Charles Wayne Goddard.

Mr. Chester Fontaine Campbell.

Then he knocked, a voice said: "Yeah? Come on in!" and Clif pushed the portal open.

Oh, it was the Camel all right! Almost the first thing Clif saw was that trick chin. He still couldn't believe that it was real and not formed of putty, for it stood forth like something thought of after the rest of the Camel had been put together. The Camel stared inquiringly, pausing in the act of applying a pair of military brushes to dampened hair.

"Goddard?" asked Clif.

"Not in. Gone to supper, I guess."

"Oh," said Clif, still looking fascinatingly at the chin, which waggled engagingly when the Camel spoke. "Well, I'll drop around later."

He started out, but the Camel was curious. "Who'll I tell him called?" he asked.

Clif smiled engagingly. "Henry Ford," he replied. Then he closed the door and went away, chuckling.

The Camel's name was Campbell; Charles—no, Chester Fontaine Camp—

Clif clutched at the stair railing. Campbell! Wasn't that pronounced Camel sometimes? Surely it was! Cambell or Camel, both ways. "The Campbells are coming!" Gosh, wasn't it a scream?

Wouldn't Loring be tickled when he heard that the Camel really was a Camel? Clif grinned and chuckled all the way back to the flivver and was still grinning when he swung about and started back toward home.

The illuminated clock said six-six as he passed the green. He wondered if he could roll the car up to the school grounds in time to make a hasty flight through West and reach the dining hall before the doors were closed. It had taken him all of forty minutes to do that twenty-six miles on the outward trip, but going back he wouldn't have to chase a tail light around the factory building in Loomis. If he hit it up pretty well he could make it, he thought.

There were fewer cars on the road now and he fairly gave the flivver its head once he was past the limits of the town. The little car complained in every joint as it bounded along, but the engine kept up a steady if agitated tune and the miles went past. Clif was a bit proud of his success, rather fancied himself as a detective. What was to come of his identification of the Camel he didn't know, but he had done his part. He rattled across the bridge at Loomis, skirted the big factory and passed through the village at a speed that would have caused the town constable acute pain had he been on hand. But the constable was probably eating supper behind one of the dimly lighted windows that whizzed by.

Frequently Clif consulted his watch and found each time that he did so that he was doing better than when he had gone in the other direction. Perhaps, he told himself with a smile, automobiles were like horses in one thing: they went faster toward home than away from it! Only three other vehicles had passed him so far; two automobiles and a farmer's wagon laden with boxes of vegetables; Clif guessed them to be cabbages. Consequently he was not overcautious as he neared one of the little hamlets a few miles beyond Loomis. There were no more than half a dozen houses and a store in it, and they stretched for many rods on each side of the road. The store was dark and few of the houses showed more than a glimmer of light. On the right stood an automobile, just beyond the store, and Clif's headlights picked it up none too soon. He swerved sharply to avoid it, and then many things happened at once. Beyond the darkened car, a second and smaller car, hidden from Clif's view, came to life and pulled abruptly into the road. Clif's first knowledge of it came when other lights suddenly blended with his on the pavements. Then the car itself loomed directly in his path. There was no time to sound his horn, no time to use his brakes effectively. There was just one thing to do and Clif did it. He wrenched hard on the steering wheel and shot over to the left. There might be room and there might not. There wasn't. The flivver went head-on into a tree.

CHAPTER XVII
MR. BINGHAM IS STERN

It was about a quarter to seven when the news reached Mr. Frost, Assistant to the Principal at Wyndham, that a boy giving his name as Bingham had been in an automobile accident at Ledyard and was now on his way to Freeburg. The informant, a woman, was vague as to the extent of the boy's injuries; but thought he was pretty badly hurt. He had been unconscious, she said, when they had picked him up. He had run his car right into a tree. No, he wasn't unconscious now; no, sir, not when her husband had started off with him. They didn't have a doctor at Ledyard; the nearest one was four miles away, at Loomis; and so they were taking the boy to Freeburg; yes, sir, to a doctor. No, she didn't know what doctor, but—

Mr. Frost hung up then and became active.

"Well, my friend, you came off pretty well," he informed Clif. "You've got a broken left clavicle and a sprained thumb. Nice, clean break, too. Any other sore places you've forgotten to mention?"

"No, sir. What's a clavicle, doctor? Collar bone?"

"Exactly." The doctor's fingers settled again on Clif's left shoulder and the boy winced. "You'll probably be rather stiff all over to-morrow, but you got out of it pretty luckily. All right. Now we'll truss you up." The doctor opened his bag wide and began to set out an appalling array of bandages and splints. "We'll have you as good as new in two or three weeks, my boy."

"Two or three weeks!" cried Clif. "Gosh, I've got to be fixed up a whole lot quicker than that, sir!"

The doctor paused in unrolling a bandage and lifted his eyebrows inquiringly. "That so? What's the hurry?"

"Why—why—I'm on the team, sir!"

"Oh." The doctor shrugged, smiled and went on with his preparations. "That's it, eh? Well, the team will just have to worry along without you for a while. Now, then, let's have this arm up here. Easy! Hold it!"

Clif agreed without enthusiasm, frowning a bit as the doctor swathed him in yards and yards of bandage. Mr. Frost said: "I'll drop a line to your father, Bingham, when I go down. I'll see you in the morning and let you explain how you came to be running about in an automobile this evening." Mr. Frost smiled as he spoke, and

Clif wasn't worried. Mr. Frost was a good scout, he reflected. He did wish, though, that his father didn't have to be informed. Dad would think him such an ass to do a thing like that! He ventured the suggestion that it might not be necessary to trouble his father with the tidings, at least not just yet, but Mr. Frost wouldn't entertain it. He went off then, and presently the doctor finished his work, wrote a prescription and gave it to Mr. McKnight and shook Clif's good hand gently.

"Gosh, I couldn't if I wanted to!" grumbled Clif.

"Well, don't want to," chuckled the doctor. "Oh, by the way, a little iodine on that goose egg there might help. Have you any?"

"Yes, sir," answered Tom. "I'll attend to it, sir." Then he added in a weak attempt at facetiousness: "That's nothing to what a fellow did to him in practice last week, doctor!"

When the two were alone, Tom seated himself gingerly on the side of Clif's bed and the two stared at each other for a long moment without a word. Then Tom shook his head dejectedly and Clif sighed. "I'm dished for this season, Tom," he muttered.

"Looks like it," Tom acknowledged. "Tough luck, old scout. Wish it had been me."

Clif considered that. Then he shook his head. "No, if one of us had to do it, it's lucky I was the one. You're a good deal more valuable to the team than I am, Tom. Does Loring know?"

"I guess so. It's all over school. I haven't seen him since supper, though."

"Maybe you'd better drop around there and tell him that I'm all right."

"I'll see him right after study hour. The gong's about due. 'Lovey' will be in again presently, Clif, and I'll be back as soon as I see Loring. Are you all right? Does it hurt a lot?"

"Here, I'll pull that pillow up a bit. That better? Well, I'll have to beat it." Tom approached the door slowly, remembered his books, came back for them and paused to stare sorrowfully at his chum.

Clif smiled. "Chase yourself, Tom. I'm all right. Oh, by the way, I forgot! Tell Loring I ran the Camel to his lair, will you?"

"You did? I'll have to hear about it when I get back!" Then the eagerness died out of Tom's voice. "Heck," he growled; "I wish Loring had never seen the coot!"

Mr. Bingham arrived at Wyndham the next afternoon, proving conclusively that Mr. Frost had performed his duty promptly. He looked very sympathetic as he sat down by Clif's bed and made anxious inquiries, but Clif had a disturbing suspicion that there was a twinkle lurking in his dad's eye. He had always been the counselor of caution, protesting against his father's recklessness on the road, and now see what had happened! He shifted restively, bringing a sharp twinge to the injured shoulder, when Mr. Bingham said: "Now tell me just what happened, son. You were driving some one's car and—"

"Did you drive over, dad?" he asked carelessly.

"Er—no. No, as a matter of fact, Clif, I didn't. You see, Mr. Frost's letter didn't reach me until eleven, and it's quite a ways by road. After all, the train does get you there fully as quick, doesn't it?"

"Not the trains on this road," answered Clif. "Not when you have to change and then stop at every telegraph pole! You'll have to think up a better alibi than that, dad!"

Mr. Bingham was frankly chuckling now. "Well, I suppose I'd better confess, son," he answered. "The reason I didn't drive is that the car isn't—that is, it needs overhauling."

"How come? It was in the shop only five weeks ago."

"Was it? It seems longer." Mr. Bingham sounded quite surprised. "How time doesn't fly, eh?"

"You'd better come clean, sir," said Clif severely. "What happened to the car?"

"How fast, dad?"

"Oh, not very fast. Maybe twenty or twenty-five. And—"

"Or maybe thirty-five. All right. Then what?"

"Why, there was one of those infernal oil wagons backing out of a side street. You know how big they are. Well, there was just about room to get around him and I'd have done it before he hit me if this other dummy hadn't been coming the other way. Really, the way some men drive is a crime, Clif! Mind you—"

"Which did you hit, dad? The oil wagon or the other one?"

"I didn't hit either of them," said Mr. Bingham indignantly. "They hit me. Both of them. At once and simultaneous."

"Geewhillickens! And you mean to say the car isn't hurt much?"

"Oh, of course it got scratched a bit. Lamps and front bumper. And one running board. And a dent in the left-hand rear door. Still, a hundred and fifty dollars will cover it. And the insurance folks will look after everything."

"What happened to you, sir?"

"Not a thing. I sat tight. I honestly think that's the best thing to do, Clif. Sit tight, eh? Now if you had sat tight last night—"

"No, no, Clif! Not *broad* daylight, really! It was getting along toward five o'clock."

"That's broad daylight," said Clif uncompromisingly. "I had my trouble when it was pitch dark! Gee, you've got a crust, dad!"

"Have I?" laughed Mr. Bingham. "But didn't I do it pretty well, son? I was more than an hour getting that speech together on the train coming up here. Had to write it on an envelope and commit it to memory—most of it. I did add a few impromptu touches, however. Now, honest, wasn't it—well, pretty fair?"

Clif's indignation held for a moment longer and then his lips trembled and after that he laughed until he had to hold on to his injured shoulder. And Mr. Bingham laughed, too, and found a cigar in his case and almost lighted it before he remembered where he was. Finally Clif sobered again.

"Just the same," he said severely, "it's no laughing matter. You're going to get smashed up some day, dad, if you don't use more sense in driving. How many times have I told you you ought to slow down at corners? Gosh, you come around a turn like there was no one else owned a car! When you can't see what's ahead of you you ought to—" But just then Mr. Bingham's grin brought him up. "Well, it's so," he ended rather lamely.

His father laughed. "Son," he said, "it looks like a tie. Let's call it off. What do you say?"

"Well, they told me six days," said Mr. Bingham. "And, look here, what about the Lizzie you were driving? Who settles for that?"

"I do," answered Clif promptly. "It's sort of folded up, like an accordion, Tom says; but they're going to pull it out again for forty dollars, and I'm going to settle out of my pocket money."

"Hm, forty dollars is a lot of money. Look here, how would it do if they only pulled it out halfway, say about twenty-five dollars' worth?"

"It isn't all for pulling it out," Clif laughed. "It got busted up pretty well, I guess."

"Well, I think you're right about paying for it yourself, son. Maybe it will teach you to be more—" But he caught the warning gleam in his son's eye and broke off with a cough. "What I started to say was you're likely to be rather hard up after settling for the wreck and so I'll just leave a little check to carry you on."

"No, sir, I don't want—"

"Of course not! I understand that. But there's Christmas coming along pretty soon—"

"Six weeks and more," jeered Clif.

"I know, but six weeks goes before you realize it." Mr. Bingham was already busy with check book and fountain pen. "I'm expecting something particularly nice from you this year and—" His voice trailed away as he tore the check from the book and waved it.

"I'm not stopping you. That check hasn't a thing in the world to do with that busted flivver, son. It's just a little present from a grateful parent."

"Grateful for what?" asked Clif suspiciously.

"Grateful to find you with nothing worse than a broken collar bone, Clifton," answered Mr. Bingham gently.

Clif looked away. Then he said, a bit gruffly: "Don't see that I ought to get the check, though. It wasn't my fault I didn't get killed."

"Some one's got to take it," replied his father lightly.

"Well, I'll use some of it for the doctor. Thanks, dad."

Mr. Bingham waved the thanks aside with a hand which again held the absent-minded cigar and laid his other hand on Clif's. "Now I'm going down for a short smoke," he said. "It's been rather a trying day, son. Then I'll come back and have supper with you."

"Up here?" exclaimed Clif incredulously.

Mr. Bingham nodded. "Little idea of my own. Rather clever, don't you think?"

"Well, but—will they let you?"

"Oh, yes, I made the suggestion to Mr. Frost and he agreed to it. Not with enthusiasm, perhaps, but—he agreed. Back in ten minutes, son."

CHAPTER XVIII
TOM HAS NERVES

Tom was extremely flattering when he returned from practice. He declared that Clif's absence from the team was universally regarded as a frightful catastrophe. He even hinted that "G. G." was on the verge of a nervous breakdown as a consequence of Clif's loss. Mr. Bingham visibly swelled with pride, but Clif told him not to be a silly ass and requested particulars of the afternoon. Well, said Tom, they had managed to pull through the scrimmage to the tune of 11 to 3. Weldon had been in Clif's place at left tackle; but, joking aside, hadn't played it for beans. Coles had had a whack at it, too, just at the end. Oh, Clif could laugh, but the old outfit had felt his loss just the same!

"Sure do miss you, Bingham," said Lemuel John in taking leave. "You were a mighty nice fellow to play against."

"Huh," laughed Clif, "you liked me because you could put it all over me!"

Lemuel John grinned and shook his head. "That ain't so, but I did feel sort of proud when I bested you once or twice. This fellow Smythe, and the other fellow—Weldon, ain't it?—aren't terribly smart, I guess. Anyway, I don't have a hard time with 'em."

Mr. Otis visited him that Friday evening during study hour. He was very sympathetic and kind, but his visit didn't make Clif any happier. Even "G. G.'s" repeated assertion that Clif's loss to the team was a genuine misfortune, while pleasing as a compliment, didn't butter any parsnips. Clif wanted to play football.

Loring came, borne by the faithful Wattles, and Clif gave a full but apathetic narrative of his adventure in pursuit of the Camel. Loring's look of incredulous delight when told that the chap's name really was Campbell got a laugh from Clif. "Have you said anything to any one about it?" Loring asked.

"Only to dad, and he didn't repeat it."

"I suppose we'd better tell Mr. Otis. He hasn't been back since. The Camel, I mean. Maybe he suspected something, eh?"

"I don't think he did," replied Clif. "I don't believe he connected me with the fellow on the road. He couldn't have seen my face very well, for it was getting pretty dark, and when I followed him to his room I put my cap in my pocket. He probably thought me one of the Wolcott bunch, or, maybe, some chap from the village."

"Well, if he should come back—" Loring paused and viewed Clif thoughtfully.

"Of course," mused the latter, "you can't make trouble for a fellow just because he comes and watches the football practice."

"Not—er—officially," agreed Loring.

"No, not officially." Then they looked at each other a moment in silence. Finally Clif smiled. Then Loring smiled.

"We'll wait a few days before we say anything to Mr. Otis, I guess," Loring said. "How is the shoulder?"

"Oh, it hurts," answered Clif. "The doctor says it's knitting. If it is, it gives me a jab every time it takes a stitch!"

"I feel pretty rotten about it," said the other. "If I hadn't started the business you wouldn't have got smeared up this way. No hope of getting back to the team, I suppose?"

"Not a mite. But you don't need to blame yourself. It was my own silly fault. I don't honestly believe I ever took a chance like that before. Of course, the road looked clear enough, but I oughtn't to have been going so fast. You see, I was so plaguey hungry! And then, confound it, when I could eat I didn't want a thing!"

"Too bad you can't see the game to-morrow."

"Rotten! Are you going over? You said last week—"

"No." Loring shook his head. "I changed my mind." He didn't state, however, that he had changed it on Clif's account. "Tell you what I thought we'd do, old chap. If you are going to be around to-morrow—" Clif nodded—"we'll get the returns by telephone in East. The booths are right near my room, you know."

"Well, but who—how—"

"There's a chap named Sanford, a junior, whom I've been helping a bit with his Latin. He's a decent kid. Sanford's agreed to call up East on the telephone after the first half and after the game's over and slip me the tidings. At least, we'll know how it's going. It will beat waiting until the crowd gets back."

"Good stunt," agreed Clif. "I'd sure like to see that game, though. Tom says no one seems very hopeful."

Loring shook his head. "I was hopeful until to-day, but every one else is so pessimistic that I'm slipping, too. I'm rather afraid that we're in for a licking. They say Horner's awfully good."

"She was last year, too." Clif shook his head gloomily. "What price 'No Defeats'?"

"I'm going to be pretty sore if we do lose," muttered the other. "Still, perhaps we'll pull through. The left side of our line isn't much, but maybe Horner won't discover it."

"Don't you fool yourself. Horner knows all there is to know, I'll bet. How much will you give me for this button, Loring?"

Loring glanced at the blue-and-white disk on Clif's lapel and smiled. "Just what it cost you," he answered. Then: "Oh, hang it, Clif, we mustn't get licked now after getting through so far!" he protested. "We've *got* to win!"

"A-a-ay!" cheered Loring.

"'No Defeats' is my motto, and long may it wave o'er the land of the free and the home of the brave!"

"Gentlemen," said Tom, entering on Clif's peroration, "I shall have to ask you to make less noise. It is requested that quiet reign after nine-thirty in order that the gallant heroes of to-morrow's battle may retire early and slumber undisturbed. I shall also have to ask you, Mr. Deane, to take your departure."

"Go to thunder," said Loring pleasantly.

"Tie that outside," advised Clif. "Where do you get all this soft pedal stuff?"

"Coach's orders," replied Tom with dignity. "After nine-thirty—"

"It isn't nine-thirty yet, you poor boob!"

"It is by my watch. At least, it's nine-twenty-eight."

"Your watch!" jeered Clif. "What good's a watch that's soaked two or three times a week?"

"This valuable and inflammable—I mean infallible timepiece has never been pawned, I'd have you know."

"No, but you take it into the bathtub regularly. How many times do you suppose you've had it under water, Tom?"

Tom grinned. "Maybe a dozen. It doesn't seem to hurt it much, though. Oh, it gains a few minutes now and then, or loses; but it still ticks on."

"How was the meeting?" asked Loring.

"Noisy. Jeff made a pretty good spiel, though."

"They didn't call on you for a speech, by any chance?" Clif inquired.

"No, and I had one all ready, too. I was going to say: 'Mr. Chairman, gentlemen and members of the faculty.'" Tom struck an attitude and stared sternly at the lamp. "'Unprepared as I am for this unexpected honor, it nevertheless gives me great pleasure to be here this evening and find before me this brilliant assemblage of beauty and gallantry. Never before in all my experience as a public speaker have I addressed a more intelligent looking audience. Even, gentlemen, when I turn and gaze upon those seated here on the platform, I still find distinct traces of—I dare not say intelligence, but of sanity. I particularly refer to those on my left, the shining-faced members of our so-called musical clubs. The others, as you will readily perceive, are football players, faculty and similar members of the lower orders; in a word, ameba. I will say—'"

"Where'd you get it?" inquired Loring. "'Ameba'! What do you know of our young friend, Clif? I believe he's looked into a dictionary!"

"Wrong. Mr. Babcock used it one day last week in hygiene. What else, Tom?"

"You've interrupted the flow of my thoughts," said Tom severely. "There was much more of it, but it has gone. I composed it while 'Pinky' Hilliard was getting off his usual drivel about 'honor before success.' It was good, too."

"Did you really sit on the platform?" asked Clif.

"What was the spirit of the meeting?" asked Loring.

"Death with honor," replied Tom, finding a peanut that hadn't been opened and gobbling the contents before Clif could formulate a protest. "Oh, we all sang and yelled hard enough, and shouted 'No Defeats!' whenever we got a chance; but, heck, every one knows we're going to get the can!"

"That's the wrong thought," said Clif. "Of course we'll get licked if you and the rest of the gang go over there to-morrow with that belief. Loring and I are optimists, Thomas. We don't know the meaning of the word defeat. We—"

"You'll know it to-morrow," answered Tom, pulling off his coat. "Lemuel John talked the same sort of rot. Stuff about 'the team that won't be beaten can't be beaten,' and all that. Some one's been feeding that baby raw milk! I'm going to bed."

"Which means that I've got to beat it," said Loring. "And my carriage wasn't to call until nine-fifty. If you want to get rid of me, Tom, you'll have to find Wattles. He's down in the library."

"Heck, I don't want to get rid of you. You won't bother me any, because I don't expect to do much sleeping before midnight. I'm willing to try, just to oblige 'G. G.,' but I know it can't be done. My sprightly little mind is far, far too active. 'Just before the battle, Mother, I—'"

"Blessed if Tom hasn't got nerves!" marveled Clif.

"I've got something," growled the accused. "You would, too, if you'd listened to 'G. G.' this evening in the gym."

"What did he say?" inquired Loring.

"Never mind," answered Tom darkly. "He said plenty. He said things no gentleman can say to another without fighting!"

"Did you fight him?" asked Clif innocently.

"Did I? I'll say I did! I knocked him down and kicked him all over the gym floor—in my mind! If we do win that blamed game to-morrow it'll be just because he told us we couldn't do it; that we haven't got the stuff in us to beat a team that knows any real football! The big stiff!"

"Well, have you?" asked Loring quietly.

Tom's head came up and he glared across belligerently, one shoe suspended in air. Then he grinned. "You wait and see," he muttered.

"Atta boy!" applauded Clif, laughing.

"Oh, I don't say we're going to beat those guys," said Tom doggedly; "but 'G. G.' isn't going to be able to tie any can to me when it's over! I'll show the fresh simp that he doesn't know what he's talking about when he says I dope *my* hair!"

"*What!* Did he say that?" exclaimed Clif.

"Yes, he did. Not me, especially, but the run of us. 'Trouble with you tea hounds,' he said, 'is that you're scared to move around much for fear you'll get the slickum off your hair!'"

"Oh, lovely!" Clif gurgled.

"I don't see anything lovely about it," protested Tom, viewing the laughing countenances of the others. "Or funny, either. 'Tea hounds,' eh? Fresh Aleck!"

"Well, Tom, you know you did work up a patent-leather finish one night in Paris," said Loring. "Maybe it still shows."

"Oh, shut up! I just tried the stuff, and you know it. Anyhow—" and Tom seemed to be struck by a sudden thought—"what if some of us do use the stuff? Don't we wear head guards?"

To Tom's puzzlement, the others again went into gales of laughter. "You make me sick," he informed them aggrievedly.

"You're so—so beautifully literal," chuckled Loring.

"I'm going to suggest," Clif laughed, "that we change that slogan to 'No Slickum!'" Wattles' appearance relieved the situation.

CHAPTER XIX
DEFEAT BY TELEPHONE

Wyndham departed early Saturday morning, valiantly shouting "No Defeats!" Team and supporters left the school together, and not for a long while had the staid old village of Freeburg listened to such a matutinal disturbance. It would be permissible to say that all Wyndham went to the game, although, if I am to be tied to facts, some two score fellows, mostly juniors, remained behind. There were no classes to-day, and after seeing the crowd off, Clif wondered what on earth he was to do with himself. He didn't feel very happy, anyway, and the prospect of an interminable morning was not cheering. Of course there was Loring, but even Loring didn't make up for what he had lost.

Being allowed to come and go as he liked about the school and village helped somewhat to-day. Of course he felt uncomfortable and awkward and was sure that he must look rather silly, and in consequence he didn't venture beyond the gates. He parted from Loring with the plea that he meant to do an hour or so of studying, and after some delay he actually did bury his nose in his books for almost that long. But his thoughts didn't take kindly to the subjects imposed on them and it was hard going. Outside, on the nearer gridiron, a handful of youngsters were kicking a football about, and their cries and the sound of the impact of shoe against pigskin came in through a half-opened window. It was such wonderful weather for football, too! A cloudy day with no wind and just a touch of frost in the still air. Clif thought his fate pretty hard.

"This is Sanford," came a distant but clear voice. "The first quarter is just over, Deane, and there's no score. We won the toss and Horner kicked off, but neither side was able to score. Can you hear me all right?"

"Yes," answered Loring. "How does it look, Charley? Who's going to win?"

"I don't know, really. You see, both teams played sort of ragged. We made a couple of fumbles and got penalized twice and Horner wasn't much better. It has just started to rain here; not hard, though; and they're saying that if the field gets wet Horner will have an advantage. She's got a whale of a team for size! I'll call up again after this quarter."

"Sorry to keep you waiting," said Sanford apologetically at the other end; "but I'm telephoning from the field house and half a dozen fellows got ahead of me. Half's over, Deane, and it's two to nothing. Horner threw Sproule for a safety."

"Oh, the dickens! How did it happen, Charley?"

"They've been going through our left side pretty hard, and just before the end of the half they tried a forward pass from our thirty, about; and Kemble got it and then it went to Sproule for a punt. Horner broke through and nailed him before he could kick."

"Well, we must be playing pretty rotten," said Loring dejectedly.

"We aren't playing so badly, really," answered the distant voice. "Horner's had all the breaks, Deane. Say, we thought we had the game once. Kemble ran from their forty-two for a touchdown. At least, we all thought it was a touchdown and nearly went crazy. Then the referee brought the ball back and we were penalized for off-side!"

"It was! And you never heard such yelling, Deane! Gosh, the crowd was sore when—Deane, there's a fellow waiting to phone and I'll have to hang up. I'll give you the final score, if I can get to a phone. So—"

"What about the field, Charley. Has it stopped raining?"

"No, but it's just sort of a Scotch mist, you know. I don't believe it'll make much difference. Well, good-by."

"Two to nothing at the end of the half," announced Loring. "Horner blocked a kick and Sproule was thrown for a safety."

The group in the hall broke into excited discussion and Loring and Clif retired once more to the room. "He said Horner was gaining through our left," reflected Loring. "That means Smythe, I suppose. Weldon, too, probably. I guess you'd have been useful over there this afternoon, Clif."

Clif sighed. "Oh, well, it isn't over yet. Even a field goal will beat two points. Gee, I'll bet Tom was fit to be tied when he found he hadn't scored that touchdown!"

"Wasn't that perfectly beastly luck? I wonder who the dumb-bell was that was off-side. Anyhow, Clif, he showed 'G. G.' that he doesn't varnish his hair!"

"We scored it and she gets it," he answered despondently.

"A safety is two points, isn't it?" inquired Wattles as he disposed of the suits on their hangers. "At what stage of the game, Mr. Loring?"

"End of the half."

"Oh, then, we've still a chance, haven't we?" Wattles brightened perceptibly. "I fancy Mr. Tom will be heard from, sir."

"He's been heard from," said Clif flatly. "He went forty-two yards for a touchdown, Wattles, but some idiot was off-side and it was no good."

"Forty-two yards! My word, sir, but that was extraordinary. I'd like to have seen it."

"I'm glad I didn't," growled Clif. "It must have been awful when they called him back."

It was almost four when the telephone rang again. Clif shook his head. "That can't be he. It isn't time for the game to be over, not by five minutes. You see what it is, Wattles."

Wattles returned in a minute. "Mr. Sanford, sir, on the wire."

"Already? It can't be over!" But Loring, with Wattles as chauffeur, made the width of the corridor in record time. "Hello, Charley! Yes? This is—"

"I see. Well, thanks awfully for phoning, Charley. Drop in soon and let me hear all about it."

"All right, Deane. Very glad to have—"

The other's voice ended abruptly and after waiting a moment Loring jiggled the phone. "Guess some one cut me off," he muttered. "Doesn't matter, though." He waited a moment longer and handed the instrument back to Clif. "Hard luck, eh?"

"They defeated us, sir?" asked Wattles anxiously.

Loring nodded. "Final score, fellows," he announced to the small audience. "Horner won, two to nothing."

Well, that was that. Clif shut the door on the sounds of disappointment that came from the recreation room, thrust his hands in his pockets and went to the window. It was already twilight outside, for the clouds had been thickening during the afternoon. Rather a dismal-looking world out there, he thought.

"'No Defeats!'" murmured Loring.

"At that," growled Clif defiantly, "I'll bet we played as well as they did! They had a lot of luck, that's all. You can't win when the other fellow's hung with horseshoes!"

"They say a lot of things," muttered Clif. "Hang it, don't start talking philosophical, Loring. I don't feel that way. Look here, where's that cross-word book of yours? Let's try one of those puzzles, will you? I don't want to think any more about that rotten game."

"Good scheme, Clif. Neither do I, I guess. I say, Wattles, find that cross-word book, will you?"

"Here it is, Mr. Loring. If you'll not be requiring me here, sir, for about a half-hour, I'd like to walk into the village before the shops close."

"Go to it, old chap. And, say, Wattles, stop at the Greek's and tell him to be sure and save us the New York papers to-morrow. We didn't get the *Times* last week."

"Chasing the emu," which was Tom's term for working out cross-word puzzles, proved absorbing enough presently to take the boys' minds off the football defeat. With Clif officiating at an abridged and sometimes inadequate dictionary, not only the emu but the roc and the moa were discovered, there was an exciting adventure with an asp and they were hot on the trail of a skink when Wattles came back. Wattles brought with him a long, unwieldy parcel from which depended an express tag, and Clif, glancing up in the very act of impaling the skink on his pencil point, voiced curiosity.

"For the love of lemons, Wattles, what have you got there?" he asked.

"Skink? How would you spell skink, for Pete's sake? *S, k, i, n, k,* skink. The *T* is silent as in 'Oolong.'"

"Well, but—"

"Beg pardon, Mr. Loring," said Wattles, withdrawing his head from the closet; "but there appears to have been a mistake about the score."

"Score?" Loring looked up a trifle blankly. "What score?"

"The score of the football game, sir. I fancy Mr. Sanford was in error."

"Huh? How come?" Clif swung about eagerly. "What did you hear, Wattles?"

"Why, sir, in the village they had it three to two, in our favor."

"Gosh!" Clif looked questioningly at Loring. Loring shook his head.

106

"They've probably got it wrong, Clif. Sanford would know best, I guess."

"Yes, but it wasn't over when he phoned! Look here, I'm going to call up and find out!"

"There's no necessity, Mr. Clifton." Wattles fumbled in a waistcoat pocket and brought forth a slip of yellow paper. "I thought I'd better make certain, and so I dropped in at the telegraph office and asked. I got the operator to write it down, Mr. Loring, so you'd know it was correct."

"Well, what was it? Hang it, Wattles, if you know anything—"

But Wattles was not to be hurried. He unfolded the slip, identified it and then laid it on the open cross-word book. Loring and Clif bent over it eagerly.

"Final," they read. "Wyndham 3, Horner 2. Carlson, Wyndham, kicked placement from forty yards just before whistle. Congratulations!"

CHAPTER XX
THE CAMEL EXPLAINS

Wyndham returned about nine o'clock, wearied but rejoicing. Very few voices had successfully stood the strain of that last moment triumph, and it was two days before the school spoke normally again. Even Tom, when he turned up at Loring's room a few minutes subsequent to his return, was decidedly hoarse. He had, he explained, talked most of the way back, like every one else, and the effort to make himself heard above the noise of the train had been too great. They made him talk some more, nevertheless—Loring and Clif—while Wattles, inventing an occupation in a corner of the room, remained to hear.

Tom wasn't a bit peeved about that lost touchdown. "Oh, well," he said, "we didn't need it, after all; and I had the fun of making the run. I was a little sore at the time, you bet; but what was the use?"

"Who was off-side?" asked Clif.

Tom looked blank. "I couldn't see," he said.

"Well, you heard, didn't you?"

"Oh, I didn't pay much attention. Forget it, Clif. He felt worse than the rest of us. Besides, it was just because he wanted to win. He was too anxious."

"Of course he didn't mean to do it," agreed Clif. "All right. What about Carlson's kick?"

"I wish I could have seen it," murmured Loring.

"So do I," sighed Clif.

That hairbreadth victory worked a swift and amazing change at Wyndham. The school had journeyed to Horner hoping, but fearing, and had returned convinced of success. Carlson's place kick was regarded as something close to a miracle, and when miracles come to your aid you can't help believing in your destiny. But Wyndham wasn't overconfident. The narrow escape had left her a bit chastened, in spite of ultimate triumph, and the general feeling was that while the prize was to be won it must be worked for. "No Defeats!" was no longer a phrase to be shouted glibly. It was no longer merely a slogan. It had become an invocation. Clif would no longer have protested had some one likened it to *On ne passe pas!* One heard it less often during the following fortnight, but when it was heard it had a deeper significance, a more earnest sound.

On Sunday the Triumvirate discussed the Camel after Tom had asked for information. He said he was surprised that they hadn't told Mr. Otis before then and insisted that the coach ought to know at once. "We thought we'd wait and see if he turned up again," said Loring. "If he's learned anything he shouldn't know it's too late now, Tom, and 'G. G.' couldn't do anything about it. But if he comes back we might—well, we might teach him a lesson."

"Sure, that's all right. Teach him all you want," responded Tom; "but Mr. Otis ought to know about it, just the same. If some of the Wolcott football crowd sent the Camel over here to spy it's well to know it. Maybe 'G. G.' would like to do something about it. I don't know what, but something."

"Maybe you're right," Loring acknowledged. "You and Clif had better go over to the inn and see him."

They did. Coach Otis was interested, but not greatly concerned. "So that's what you were up to when you got that busted collar bone, eh?" he asked Clif. "Next time you'd better come to me and let me handle it. What that fellow learned from watching our practice can't be much, and certainly not nearly so serious as losing a good lineman just when he's most needed. If you or Deane see him around again let me know and I'll have a talk with him. I hardly think he's been sent by the football team or the coach over there. More likely he's doing it on his own hook, with some silly notion that he's going to make some important discovery. Can't imagine what, though. He must know that we don't prepare for Wolcott until a couple of weeks beforehand, and that when we do we keep practice secret. To-morrow will be about his last chance of getting into the stand, so pass the word to Deane to keep his eyes peeled, will you?"

"Mr. Babcock sent me over here," he explained, "so I guess it's all right. I ain't—haven't spoken to any one about it, and maybe I'd ought to." He ended questioningly. It wouldn't be fair to say that Lemuel John looked frightened, for somehow you couldn't associate fear with him, but he certainly did look awed. Tom shook his head.

"Sit tight," he advised. "'G. G.' knows you're here and he will let you know when he wants you. Going to play guard?"

"Well, I don't know," answered the big chap. "I guess so. Ain't much else I could do, is there?"

"Yes," replied Clif after a moment's search. "That's he, all right. Guess I'd better tell 'G. G.'"

"Yes, but don't let him see you point him out. He might get scared and beat it."

Clif had to wait several minutes before a chance to communicate with the coach occurred. Then he gave his message and cautiously located the Camel in the stand. But Mr. Otis was too far away to see him. Also, he was much too busy to waste time in the effort.

"Hang the fellow!" he said impatiently. "I can't talk to him now, Bingham. Look here, you go up there and see what he's up to. Take some one with you." Mr. Otis glanced along the bench. "Take that big fellow, Parker."

"Parks, sir?"

"All right. Take him. Make that sneak talk, Bingham. Find out who sent him over here, and why. I wouldn't—better not make any trouble, you understand. Unless he won't answer questions, that is."

Clif beckoned to Lemuel John and passed around to the back of the stand where two stairways arose. On the way he put his companion in possession of the main facts of the case. "He will talk, I guess, Parks; but if he doesn't we'll have to make him. Then it's up to you, for I couldn't make a pig squeal tied up this way!"

"Sure," said Lemuel John. "I'll persuade him."

"Hello," he said.

"Hello," muttered the Camel.

"You're a long way from home, aren't you?"

The Camel turned then and got a fair view of the questioner. Recognition dawned and the puttylike chin trembled agitatedly. For a moment he seemed to be contemplating flight, but his first glance to the left revealed Lemuel John observing him calmly but interestedly past the pillar, and the idea vanished. He returned his gaze to the field. "No, I'm not," he muttered.

"Well, I suppose it doesn't take you long," said Clif. "How's Goddard?"

"All right." The Camel moved restively. Then he broke out, weakly defiant, with: "Say, what's the idea? What do you want, anyway?"

Neighbors were observing them curiously now. There was something up, that was plain, and they wanted to be in on it. Clif laughed good-naturedly. "Why, all I want is a little information,

Campbell. Suppose we go down where we can talk without being overheard."

"No!" The Camel was emphatic. "You talk right here."

"I think it would be better if the others didn't hear," insisted Clif gently. "They might—well, they might not like it; and if they didn't—" He left the rest to the Camel's imagination. After a moment's consideration the Camel said: "All right, but you haven't anything on me, and if you get funny I'll—I'll—" Then he saw Lemuel John again and stopped for good.

They went down to the back of the stand, the Camel sandwiched between Clif and Lemuel John. Above, a line of faces stared down at them. Clif led the way to the farther end of the structure. "Now," he said, his jesting manner gone, "let's hear all about it. Who sent you over here, Campbell?"

"No one sent me. I just came to—I wanted to see you fellows play football."

"We appreciate that, but why not stay at Wolcott and watch your own team? If you're not an absolute idiot, Campbell, you know that you're in wrong here. If we passed the word back to that crowd up there you'd be in for a peck of trouble." The Camel, already distinctly uneasy, looked nervous. "Now we know that you haven't been coming all the way from Cotterville two and three times a week just for amusement. We want to know who sent you, Campbell, and we mean to find out. So you'd better come clean if you know what's best for you."

"Oh, no, he isn't," said Clif. "Your quarter back is Monroe."

"Yes, but Goddard's trying, too. He's played two or three games."

"Oh, a sub, eh? All right, go ahead."

"He said it would help him if he knew something about—about—" The Camel hesitated and glanced doubtfully at Lemuel John. Lemuel John was in togs and loomed very large. "Well, if he knew the sort of game Wyndham played. Because he's pretty sure to play quarter back part of the game, and if he handled the team well—"

The Camel sort of ran down then. Clif nodded. "I see. You were to come over here and watch our fellows play and tell Goddard all you could find out so that he'd know what he was up against if he got a chance in the big game. Very pretty, Campbell. Your idea, you say?"

The Camel nodded, watching the faces of the others anxiously. Clif looked at Lemuel John. "What do you think?" he asked.

"He's lying," said the other calmly. "This Goddard got him to do it."

"He didn't!" protested the Camel. "I offered to! Really, I did!"

"Why?" asked Clif.

"Because—" the Camel's gaze fell.

"Because Goddard's your chum and you wanted to see him do well against our crowd and, maybe, make quarter back's position next year?" The Camel nodded again. "But you knew you were doing something that wasn't fair, didn't you? You knew that that sort of thing wasn't sporting?"

"I suppose I did," muttered the boy.

"If Goddard didn't put you up to it, at least he knows you're doing it. On the whole I think Goddard's the more to blame. How about it, Parks?"

"Sure. Dirty rat, I'll say." The Camel looked resentful, but Lemuel John hadn't dwarfed any since last viewed and the Camel swallowed his emotion.

"Well," resumed Clif, after a moment's consideration, "I guess you'd better run along, Campbell. I'll report this to our coach and he will do whatever he thinks best. But I don't want to ever see you around here again. Get that? If you ever put your nose inside these grounds it will be the worse for you. We'll walk along with you and see that you don't lose your way going out."

They waited until the Camel had disappeared around the corner of Oak Street and then hurried back to the gridiron. "I guess," said Clif on the way, "he told the truth, don't you?"

"I guess so, the poor chump," agreed Clif.

Mr. Otis was on the point of sending out a search party for Lemuel John when they got back to the bench, evidently having forgotten that he had detailed him for Clif's mission. "Where on earth have you been, Parker—Parks?" he demanded. "You're not supposed to leave the bench in the middle of practice! Get in there and see what you can do. Left guard. No, no, the other squad! You'd better show something if you want to stick around here, son!"

Lemuel John went off as directed, offering no excuse, while Clif reported to Loring. The latter was inclined to be sympathetic toward the Camel. "It's Goddard we ought to get after," he said. "Trying to swipe our secrets is bad enough, but getting that poor boob to do the dirty work is worse. Have you told Mr. Otis?"

"Not yet. Just have a look at him. Does he strike you as a—as an approachable sort of guy?"

He didn't. He was tagging the squad of which Braley was quarter and Lemuel John left guard, and his voice came across the field in decidedly irascible tones! Clif shook his head gently.

"If you don't mind," he murmured, "I'll wait until he has calmed down a mite."

"Oh, that's all right, sir. But doesn't it seem as though Goddard ought to get called down, at least? I mean, it was sort of a dirty trick, and he oughtn't to get off so easy."

"Bingham," replied Mr. Otis, "you'll learn by the time you're a little older that those things sort of look after themselves. You think that if we let Goddard get away with this he will escape the penalty. But he won't, my boy. Fellows who do that sort of thing provide their own punishment. I've seen it over and over. Bingham, the punishment the law inflicts on us is mighty trivial alongside what we inflict on ourselves!"

Clif departed not wholly satisfied. What Mr. Otis had said might be quite true, but so far, he reflected, the only punishment sustained by any of the actors in the recent little drama had fallen to the lot of the innocent. He couldn't quite discern why he should have a busted shoulder blade and Goddard and the Camel should get off scot-free!

Lemuel John Parks must have satisfied Mr. Otis as to his right to remain with the first team, for he stayed on the squad, received a flattering amount of attention from the coaches and seriously threatened Breeze's title of first substitute left guard. Lemuel John was all that could be desired of size, strength and willingness. If he had had a year of football experience behind him he would have ousted Smythe beyond a doubt. But Lemuel John, although he listened with almost painful intentness to the coaches and tried very, very hard, was undeniably lacking in technic. Effort, no matter how intense, will fail of its objective if wrongly applied. Yet Lemuel John made progress, and Mr. Otis recognized promising material for another year and said so to Loring one afternoon. Loring, although not officially connected with the team, was a privileged person and as such admitted past the dead-line of patroling Juniors whose proud duty it was to keep the public out of the stand and at a respectable distance from the gridiron.

"Deane," said "G. G." "you've really got a good eye for talent. That big fellow is quite as promising as you said and you did us a real service when you discovered him. I only wish we had gotten hold of him earlier!"

"Well, I didn't really discover him, Mr. Otis," answered Loring. "All I did—that is, the three of us—was to persuade him to report to Mr. Babcock. I'm glad you think he will make good, sir, for I think so, too. Next year he ought to be a corking good lineman, oughtn't he?"

"Yes, I think so, Deane. He's not so bad right now. If only he knew a little more, I'd—" Mr. Otis pursed his lips, frowned and strode off quickly. "Cotter! *Cotter!* Do that just once more if you want to quit the team! That wasn't your man! You knew it wasn't! Jackson, let's have that again. Now let me see you do that right, Cotter!"

CHAPTER XXI
LORING TAKES A WALK

C lif got rid of some of his splints and bandages on Tuesday, although he still had to carry his arm in a sling. That afternoon Dan Farrell, the trainer, stopped to inquire about the injury and remained to talk for a few minutes with Clif and Loring. Presently Loring asked: "You're going to let Clif in for a while next Saturday, aren't you, Dan?"

"Me? Sure, I won't stop him. It's up to the coach, my boy. He'll run him in for a bit, likely. But, listen, Bingham, keep that shoulder down if you play."

"Would it get broken again?" asked Clif.

"No, it's as good as ever it was, or it will be Saturday. But there'd be no sense in taking chances. If I was you I'd find me a harness and wear it; that is, if you think you'll be playing any."

"A harness? Where would I get one, Dan? Say, look here, if I had a good heavy pad on this shoulder why couldn't I play all right?"

"Why, that'll be fine," said Clif. "If there's any expense, Dan, you must let me—"

"Expense! Where would there be? The little man won't be asking me money for a few stitches. If he does I'll beat him up with his own hammer! Stop over after practice and let me study the build of you, my boy."

"Wind the cat and put the clock out," murmured Tom sleepily. "And call me early, mother dear, for I'm to be—to be—"

Then came a gentle snore.

Meetings of the Triumvirate were few that week. Once, on Wednesday, Clif and Tom stopped at Loring's room, after supper, on their way to the gymnasium. Usually the door was ajar, but now it was tightly closed, and when, after a brief knock, Tom tried to open it it was found to be also locked. From beyond it came the voices of Loring and Wattles.

"Just a minute, fellows!"

"One moment, please!"

Tom looked at Clif, slightly puzzled. "What's the idea?" he muttered. From inside came various sounds suggesting haste. Then the door was opened by Wattles. "Yes, sir, come in, please, Mr. Tom. Good evening, Mr. Clifton." Wattles sounded a trifle breathless, Clif thought. Loring had a paper on his knees and the room looked as usual.

"What's going on in here?" demanded Tom suspiciously.

"Going on?" repeated Loring. "What do you mean?"

"Oh, well, locked door." Tom waved toward the portal. "Mysterious sounds. Wattles looking foxy. Yes, you are, Wattles; decidedly foxy! Come clean, Loring. Where's the body hidden?"

But Loring declared that no murder had been committed, and, since their time was short, the visitors didn't pursue the inquiry further. In fact, they didn't think of it again until Friday night.

The last real work of the season was held Thursday, and on Friday the school, lately barred from the gridiron, paraded in force and watched the first and second take part in a brief scrimmage that was mostly all punting. After that the second disbanded, cheering themselves and the first team and Mr. Babcock and, finally, themselves once more, and romped off the field with much dancing and horse play. The first team players disappeared by ones and twos toward the gymnasium, a squad of second substitutes ran through signal drill and then it was over save for the shouting. That lasted until every member of the squad, the coach, the assistant coaches, the managers, the trainer and the team had been cheered, and only ended outside the gymnasium entrance with one last mighty "long cheer, fellows, with nine Wyndhams!"

And so, amazingly sudden, the eve of battle arrived.

Clif and Tom came back from the gymnasium about twenty minutes to eight, after a brief session before the blackboard. There was to be another drill in the forenoon and to-night Mr. Otis had been lenient. The two had promised Loring to drop in on him if they returned before study hour and so they turned in at East Hall and Tom rapped on the closed door: one ... one, two; the Triumvirate's particular signal. Once more Wattles' voice came forth.

"One moment, please!"

Tom turned to Clif and shook his head. "I smell a mystery," he muttered. "If it was Christmas Eve, now—"

But just then the door was pulled open and Tom lapsed into silence. Halfway across the room stood Loring. No, that isn't exactly so, for he didn't stand, but to the amazed regard of the two in the doorway he seemed to. At least, he was erect, and never before had Clif or Tom seen him so. Under each armpit was a crutch, and the toe of one foot rested on the floor. The other foot was held poised, as if to aid in the difficult feat of balancing. Having opened the door, Wattles swiftly returned to Loring, hovering about him anxiously. Any one well acquainted with Tom could have foretold his next words.

"*My sainted Aunt Jerusha!*" exclaimed Tom slowly, awedly, incredulously.

Loring chuckled, and, chuckling, swayed precariously. Wattles sprang forward, but Loring recovered his equilibrium. The visitors came slowly in, as though expecting the spectacle to vanish into thin air if they moved precipitately, and Clif closed the door gently behind him and leaned on it.

"My first public appearance," said Loring somewhat excitedly. "Semipublic, that is. I'm going to use these things to-morrow, and I wanted you chaps to see them first. I'm not very expert yet. Wattles has heart failure, almost, whenever I try them!"

"You do very well indeed, sir," said Wattles, watching anxiously.

"So the doctor says. Of course, I'm supposed to start off pretty slowly, Clif. A few minutes a day at first."

"Sacred Ibis of the River Nile!" murmured Tom, all eyes. It was his second-choice invocation, and its use proved that he was gradually recovering. "Crutches, by gum! What ... do ... I ... know?"

"All ready for the great exhibition, Wattles?" asked Loring.

"Yes, sir," answered Wattles nervously.

"Let's go then!" Loring advanced one crutch, set his heel lightly to the floor, advanced the other. It was a slow and halting progress he made, a series of hitching maneuvers that looked painfully difficult, but he finally reached the other end of the room, Wattles close behind him, and his arms half advanced.

"Great!" said Clif.

"I'll be dingfoozled!" breathed Tom.

"It was the crutches Wattles brought back that day I was here," said Clif. "That long bundle. Loring, it's just wonderful!"

"Well, if you think so," answered Loring, "how about me? All right, Wattles. We'll call it a day. No encores to-night. Gosh, the old chair feels pretty good again! I wonder if I'll really ever put this away in the attic." He patted the arms of the wheel chair as he spoke. "It's been a pretty good pal!" He looked whimsically at the crutches of which Wattles had relieved him and shook his head.

"Clever contraptions, Wattles old chap, but I don't feel at home with them yet!"

"No, sir; very likely, sir," said Wattles. "I fancy it will require some time, Mr. Loring, to become fully accustomed to them, but I predict, sir, that you'll have no use for the chair by spring."

"Spring?" mused Loring. He shook his head. "Wattles, you're an optimist!"

Tom, fully recovered from his surprise, spouted questions now. When had Loring known first about the crutches? How long had he had them? Would he be able to go up and downstairs on them? Didn't it make his legs feel funny to hang 'em down like that? Was he really going to use them to-morrow when he went out?

"I'm so glad, Loring," he declared earnestly, "I can't say it. I—I— Come on, Clif!"

Outside, hurrying toward the staircase, Tom blew his nose, startlingly loud. Well, for that matter, Clif felt a trifle sniffly himself.

At half-past one Clif and Tom went across to the gymnasium and changed into togs, some of the last to arrive there. Clif sought Dan and had the shoulder protector strapped and laced into place. He had had the use of his arm for several days now and, although Mr. Otis had not been consulted, Clif hoped that the formidable appearing contrivance of brown leather and gray felt would suggest to the coach that he was able to take more than a merely incidental part in the day's proceedings.

"It's Loring Deane!" some one shouted. "On crutches!"

The cheer that went up was not evoked by the white-sweatered cheer leaders. It was a wholly spontaneous roar that grew in volume as Loring came hitching onward over the turf. Not even the cheer which had greeted the team had been louder. Megaphones, flags, caps waved. The stand was on its feet, incredulous but delighted, shouting congratulations, encouragement.

"Good boy, Deane!" "Keep a-coming!" "A-a-a-ay, Deane!" "Attaboy!" "Deane! Deane! Deane!"

Loring kept a-coming and Wattles followed a stride behind, his long arms ready to go to the rescue if his charge stumbled. It is doubtful if Wattles even heard that cheering and shouting, so intent was he. And then, at last, Loring reached the big car, Wattles took the crutches and the long journey was over. Settling down between his father and his mother, Loring smiled proudly but tiredly. "I did it," he said rather faintly. He looked at his father. "The fellows seemed—pleased, I thought, dad," he said.

Mr. Sanford Deane nodded. "Sounded that way," he answered huskily. Then he, too, blew his nose quite startlingly.

An outsider, a person not sympathetically interested in either the Dark Blue or the Brown, would doubtless have found those fifty minutes tame and uninteresting. He might even have said, and without fear of successful contradiction, that the contending teams played at times no better than mediocre football. There were three fumbles in the half, of which two were accredited—or discredited—to Wyndham, and each team lost twenty yards through penalties. Several opportunities were wasted, by Wyndham and Wolcott both, and more than once signals were muddled by the quarter backs. But this was preparatory school football and not a college game, and the supposititious outsider would doubtless have recalled the fact and been lenient in his criticisms. I can be no less.

In the gymnasium five coaches talked earnestly amidst the confusion of sounds, and just before the intermission was over Mr. Otis had his say to the whole team. He didn't say much and he didn't scold once. He scarcely uttered a word of criticism now. The first half had contained some mistakes, he said, but that was what a first half was for; to get the bad football out of the system! Now all they had to do was go back there and, profiting by former errors, win the game! Wolcott, he declared, was an overrated team. If she wasn't she would have had the game tucked safely away before this. They must get rid of the idea that Wolcott couldn't be knocked down and trampled on, for she could. It would take a better team to do it, but the team was right here.

"I want a score in each of these periods, Wyndham. Give me two scores and I'll promise you a victory. Keep your eyes open and your heads up. When you tackle, tackle for keeps. Charge low and keep on going, you linemen. And all of you—" Mr. Otis' fist shot out—"*fight!*"

CHAPTER XXII

"HOLD 'EM, WYNDHAM!"

Clif found himself beside Lemuel John when he got back to the bench. Lemuel John was enjoying—enduring would be a better word—his first big game as a player, and he was considerably wrought up. For that matter, so was Clif, and Clif was not exactly a tyro. The usual ecstatic cheering died down and Carlson sent the ball away on a long journey into the south. Wolcott was unable to advance by rushing from her seventeen and punted to Wyndham's forty-six. The Dark Blue revealed her campaign then and there by returning the kick on first down. The Brown's safety man was caught napping and chased the ball over the line. From the twenty Wolcott reeled off six around Drayton back at left end, and made it first down on the next try when the whole backfield concentrated on Breeze. But a second attempt to negotiate the enemy's left end failed, and, after two thrusts at Cotter, Wolcott again punted from her thirty-seven.

Smythe was sent back to left guard and Tom relieved Stiles. A minute later, after Wolcott had smashed once at the defenders' center, Longwell replaced Cotter after the latter had failed to respond to Dan Farrell's first-aid treatment. Cotter was helped off to a loud cheer from the stand. Wolcott got four yards on two attempts at the line and then shot her full back past Williams for three more, taking the ball to the twenty-three. A tall half back retreated to the thirty-five yards and surveyed a rather difficult angle. The Wolcott quarter knelt on the thirty-two and patted the sod smooth. Cries of "*Block that kick!*" drowned the signals as the ball shot back. The pass was good and the quarter quickly and deftly cocked the pigskin, but the wind was still a factor and the ball started away with too much elevation and, after pausing undecidedly in the air, descended well short of the goal line and to the right of the posts. And when it came down Tom was under it.

An instant later Clif was on his feet, waving his arms as well as that shoulder pad would allow him to and shouting at the top of his lungs. And Lemuel John was shaking both clenched fists at the speeding runner and talking pure Wyoming at him. After all, it was rather simple, that run of Tom's. For only a moment at the beginning of the race was the outcome in doubt. He was almost stopped by a Wolcott tackle before he had found his stride, but after that, while a hastily formed interference cut a path for him, and when the interference had been left behind, he had a clear field to the Wolcott goal line. He was pursued all the way by the enemy's fleetest runners, but he ran the race of his life and at the end of it a clear ten yards separated him from the nearest adversary.

Wyndham stood on her feet and went wild, stark, staring crazy, and the cheer leaders shouted and waved in vain. The pandemonium that was let loose had neither rhythm nor coherence, but it was whole-souled and prodigious! After a while the leaders did manage to evoke several thunderous pæans, the final one waning a trifle toward the end as Houston prepared for the try-for-point. Wolcott was savage and desperate and Houston's foot never touched the ball. The whole Wyndham left side caved in and the Brown poured through the breach. But six points looked very large just then and Wyndham was triumphant.

Wyndham now had only to defend, but that might prove no easy task, for Wolcott had the wind behind her and would play with the desperation of a team who has all to gain and nothing to lose. Wyndham chose to kick off and Carlson sent the ball low and far. But the Dark Blue ends couldn't cover that kick and a Wolcott back made twelve yards after the catch. The Brown uncovered everything she had then, and she had several things unsuspected of the adversary. One was a reverse play in which the quarter back, with a tackle preceding him, ran wide around the short end, the attack being apparently aimed the other way. Wolcott used this to advantage until, after many yards had been lost, Wyndham solved it. Wolcott ripped through Smythe and inside Weldon, found a weak spot at Williams until that youth was relieved in favor of Wells and twice used short forward heaves for five- and six-yard gains. It took Wolcott eight minutes to reach the Dark Blue's thirty-four yards, and there the tide was turned.

Wyndham tried the Wolcott left tackle for a scant yard and then punted. The punt went too high for the best results and the wind shortened it, bringing it down just beyond midfield. And from there, with some six minutes remaining, Wolcott launched her final and supreme offense.

"Goddard," he said.

Wolcott went on desperately, retrieving her loss and three yards more by an unexpected and well-worked double pass that put her on the defenders' thirty-one. From there to the twenty she smashed four times at Smythe, and when the referee waved to the linemen Smythe was of very little present use. Greene took his place, and at the same time Clif went in for Weldon. "You've been asking for it all the afternoon," said "G. G." dryly. "Go ahead and show me. Dan says you can stand the gaff, but I'd save that bad shoulder all I could."

Wolcott had one down left with which to reach the ten yards and she used it in trampling over Greene, and again the chain was moved on. Clif had forgotten that he wore a shoulder pad, forgotten that he had ever had a broken collar bone. He remembered little except that his back was close to the last white line and that Wolcott must not reach it. Sim Jackson was fairly beside himself, croaking supplications and insults almost in a breath. Captain Ogden, ready to drop, reeled weakly down the line, thumping backs and pleading hoarsely. Clif found himself saying "No Defeats! No Defeats!" over and over as he dug his cleats anew and settled himself.

From further down the field came an unceasing wave of sound. Over and over and over it boomed, deep, measured, imploring: "*Hold 'em, Wyndham! Hold 'em, Wyndham! Hold 'em, Wyndham!*"

The enemy surged again, the lines met, writhed and struggled for a long moment. Then the whistle shrilled and the referee emerged from the confusion. "Second down! About seven!"

Almost three yards that time, thought Clif in dismay as he crawled to his feet again. They had come straight at him and he had failed! Something hurt horribly somewhere, but he hadn't time to think of that. Wolcott was giving signals again. No, a whistle had blown. Some one was coming on. For whom? Gosh, it was Lemuel John! Wyndham was cheering now: "Rah, rah, rah, Parks!" "Rah, rah, rah, Greene!" Yes, Greene was out, and here was Lemuel John, pale, earnest and startlingly big. Clif took heart. If only the enemy would smash at left guard now!

But the enemy didn't. A back slid off to the left and when the dust of battle had settled the ball was close to the four yards. Almost three yards at a time! Lemuel John could talk now, and he did. "Back yonder they're telling us to hold 'em, fellows!" shouted the big fellow. "What do you say we do it? What have they got we ain't? Not a thing, pardners! Come on and heave 'em back!"

"That's the stuff!" croaked Sim Jackson. "Don't let 'em have another inch, Wyndham! Hold 'em! You can do it! I'm telling you you can! *Won't* you hold 'em, fellows?"

And from the stand came the measured slogan again, "*Hold 'em, Wyndham!*"

"Try again, young feller," said Lemuel John.

And Wolcott tried again, while the Wyndham stand still laughed ecstatically, tried and failed utterly when a back sped the ball over the line in a last desperate effort to conquer and Captain Jeff smote it mightily to earth!

* * * *

"Thought I'd drop in and see did you get damaged much," drawled Lemuel John as he came into Loring's room and faced the Triumvirate after supper that evening. He looked at Clif as he ended his statement.

"Not badly," smiled Clif. "I thought the pesky thing was busted again, but 'Doc' says no. He said things unfit for publication, though, and asked me right to my face if I was—well, a particularly profane kind of a fool!"

"Bet you couldn't answer that," chuckled Tom.

"Well, I didn't know," said Lemuel John, accepting Loring's invitation and easing his big frame onto the edge of a chair. "I saw you looked sort of pained when I got there and I heard afterwards that you'd hurt the shoulder again."

Lemuel John smiled and shook his head. "You're kidding, I guess. I didn't do anything. Didn't have any chance to. I just fooled with that kid a bit because I thought our fellows sort of needed a laugh. They was—were all sort of excited, you know; kind of wrought-up like; and I was scared they'd let those other fellows push that ball over before they'd got hep to the fact that the other fellows wasn't any better than they was—were—was?" Lemuel John looked helplessly at Loring.

"Were," said Loring gravely.

"Yeah. Well, that's all there was to that. Guess folks did get a good laugh, but, shucks, 'twasn't anything to do."

"Wasn't it?" said Clif. "Well, it did the trick, just the same. Those murderers were on their way to a touchdown, and no mistake!"

"I'll say they were," agreed Tom. "I was just closing my eyes so as not to see the tragedy. And another thing, fellows: if Wolcott had got that score she'd certainly have won, because that left half of hers hasn't missed but one 'try' this season. Lemuel John, you're a poor little half portion, and oughtn't to be allowed to take part in such a strenuous pastime as football, but you sure saved the old game!"

"Oh, shucks," muttered Lemuel John.

www.ingramcontent.com/pod-product-compliance
Lightning Source LLC
Chambersburg PA
CBHW011437170626
46808CB00009B/3080